Remember?

Remember I said, *One day, we'll be together again?*
I know that day is taking a lot longer to come than
it should, but I still believe it's gonna get here,
Little Sister. And that's why I'm trying to write
you lots and lots. Because I love writing and I
love you and when me and you are together again,
I'm gonna want us to remember everything that
happened when we were living apart. I'm gonna
hold on to all these letters and when we're living
together again, they're gonna be the first present
I give you. A whole box of the Before Time. That's
what this is, Lili, even though I know when me
and you get sad, all we think about is the other
Before Time—before the fire, before we lived apart
from each other. But this is a whole new Before
Time. And it's cool because we'll be able to
remember a whole other set of good things, right?
So I'm writing. And I'm remembering. For me.
And for you, Lili.

ALSO BY JACQUELINE WOODSON

JACQUELINE WOODSON

PEACE, LOCOMOTION

PUFFIN BOOKS

PUFFIN BOOKS

An imprint of Penguin Random House LLC, New York

First published in the United States of America by G. P. Putnam's Sons,
an imprint of Penguin Random House LLC, 2009
Published by Puffin Books, an imprint of Penguin Random House LLC, 2010

Visit us online at penguinrandomhouse.com

THE LIBRARY OF CONGRESS HAS CATALOGED THE G. P. PUTNAM'S SONS EDITION AS FOLLOWS:
Woodson, Jacqueline.
Peace, Locomotion / Jacqueline Woodson.
p. cm.
Summary: Through letters to his little sister, who is living in a different foster home,
sixth-grader Lonnie, also known as "Locomotion," keeps a record of their lives
while they are apart, describing his own foster family, including his foster
brother who returns home after losing a leg in the Iraq War.
ISBN 978-0-399-24655-5 (hc)
[1. Foster home care—Fiction. 2. Brothers and sisters—Fiction. 3. Orphans—Fiction.
4. Peace—Fiction. 5. African Americans—Fiction. 6. Letters—Fiction.] I. Title.
PZ7.W868Pe 2009 [Fic]—dc22 2008018583

Puffin Books ISBN 9780142415122

Printed in the United States of America

19 20 18

For Tashawn and Ming
And eventually, for Ryleigh

Imagine Peace

I think it's blue because that's my favorite color.

I think it's soft like flannel sheets in the
  wintertime.

I think Peace is full—
  like a stomach after a real good dinner—
  beef stew and corn bread or
  shrimp fried rice and egg rolls.

Even better

Than some barbecue chicken.

I think Peace is pretty—like my sister, Lili.

And I think it's nice—like my friend Clyde.

I think if you imagine it, like that
  Beatles guy used to sing about?

Then it can happen.

Yeah, I think

Peace Can Happen.

-Lonnie Collins Motion,
aka Locomotion

Dear Lili,

As you know, in a few days I'm going to be twelve. That means two things:
1. In six weeks, you'll be nine.
2. In nine more years, I'll be twenty-one and then I'll be old enough to take care of you by myself. And when I'm twenty-one and you're eighteen, I'll still be your big brother and kind of like the boss of you. But I won't be mean. And if you want, we can keep living in Brooklyn. Maybe we'll even find a place near your foster mama's house because I know you like it a lot over there since it's right near the park and there's a cool playground and stuff. When we're together again, I'll take you to that playground myself so you won't be missing it. Even if we're big, we can still go, right? I see big kids at the one over here sometimes. They hang off the jungle gym and go down the slide. They be acting all crazy and having a real good time.

When we were small, Mama used to take us to the playground over by where our old house was. Since you were still real little, she'd have to go with you down the slide. "Lonnie, you take your sister down the slide now," she'd say sometimes.

And even though I felt kind of stupid doing that with my friends there watching and singing, *Lonnie gotta baby-sit, Lonnie gotta baby-sit,* I did it anyways because Mama would get that smile on her face. Daddy used to say, "That's a smile make a regular man climb Kilimanjaro."

Back then, I didn't even know what Kilimanjaro was. Now I do though. It's a mountain in Africa. And if Mama and Daddy were alive and we were still little kids, I'd take you down that slide a hundred times. And climb Kilimanjaro if Mama asked me to.

Love,

Your brother to the
highest mountain,
Locomotion

Dear Lili,

This morning, when I got up and saw the rain still
coming down, I sat on the couch watching it for a
long, long time, thinking about you and Mama
and Daddy. Thinking about when we was all
together and we'd do things like take the bus to
the Prospect Park Zoo and take the train to Coney
Island. Or like when me and Daddy used to go to
the Mets games and everybody would always be
asking us how come we liked the Mets when the
Yankees was the ones always winning. I remember
Daddy said, "Ain't it boring to always be
winning?" And I thought about that for a long
time even though I was just a little kid. I thought
about how if you walk out on the field or the
basketball court or the handball court already
knowing you got the game in the bag, what's the
point? Like when me and Angel and Lamont and
Clyde be playing ball and we get some in and miss

some—well, like when that ball finally goes through that net and you hear that *swoosh!* sound and your homeboys be slapping your back and saying "good shot" and stuff? If you knew that was coming, you wouldn't even get that good feeling you get when it happens. You'd just be all regular and not caring and stuff. But when I was a little kid, I'd just say, "Winning's fun and I *sure* wish the Mets would win a little bit more!" Daddy used to laugh that big laugh of his and hug me so hard I couldn't even feel my breath moving through my lungs.

Felt real good, Lili.

Locomotion

Dear Lili,

Every day, the memories get a little bit more faded out of my head and I try to pull them back. It's like they used to be all colorful and loud and everything. They're getting grayer though. And sometimes even the ones that used to be loud get real, real quiet.

Lili, do you remember? There was a time when all of us were together. There was a time before the fire and before nobody wanted to be my foster mama until Miss Edna came along. There was a time before your foster mama came and said, "I'll take the little girl but I don't want no boys." You were the little girl, Lili. And you didn't want to go. It was raining that day just like it's raining now. And you held on to me and cried and cried. You kept saying, *I want to be with my brother.*

And I hope you know that I wanted to be with you too. But I didn't want you living in a group home anymore. I wanted you in a nice house with nice people and not kids everywhere taking your stuff and being mean to you.

Remember I said, *One day, we'll be together again*? I know that day is taking a lot longer to come than it should, but I still believe it's gonna get here, Little Sister. And that's why I'm trying to write you lots and lots. Because I love writing and I love you and when me and you are together again, I'm gonna want us to remember everything that happened when we were living apart. I'm gonna hold on to all these letters and when we're living together again, they're gonna be the first present I give you. A whole box of the Before Time. That's what this is, Lili, even though I know when me and you get sad, all we think about is the other Before Time—before the fire, before we lived apart from each other. But this is a whole new Before Time. And it's cool, because we'll be able to remember a whole other set of good things, right? So I'm writing. And I'm remembering. For me. And for you, Lili.

Love,

Locomotion

Dear Lili,

I know it's been three years since that day when your foster mama came. But the way I figure it— me and you are both gonna live to be at least a hundred years old and given that fact—three years, four years, even if it takes nine years—well, that's not a real, real long time after all.

Love you to eternity,

Locomotion

Dear Lili,

Today in school we got the good news that
Ms. Cooper is going to be leaving soon. Her belly's
been growing a lot since school started but
nobody in class liked her enough to ask if that was
a baby inside. Not even LaTenya and LaTenya likes
everybody. On the first day of school, I told
Ms. Cooper I was a poet since last year Ms. Marcus
told me that's what I should call myself because
she said my poems were real good. I liked saying
I'm a poet a whole lot and every time I say it to
Rodney or Miss Edna, they always say *You sure
are, so just keep on writing those poems, Lonnie.* But
when I said it to Ms. Cooper, she just looked at me
and folded her arms. Then she asked me if I'd
published any books. I said not yet, since I'm only
in sixth grade and all. But I told her I wanted to
publish a whole lot one day. Ms. Cooper just gave
me her back and walked over to her desk. She

said, "Until you publish a book, you're not a poet, you're an *aspiring* poet, Lonnie." So after that I went back to being just a regular boy—not a poet like Ms. Marcus had said. I don't think Ms. Marcus had been lying. I guess there's just people that think you're a good poet and people who don't really care about poetry and the people who like to write it. I still write a few poems but mostly I'm writing these letters to you, Lili. It's not like I believe Ms. Cooper—it's just that she made me feel a little stupid for thinking I was really a poet. I hate that feeling. And plus, the very next day after she said that, I got a forty-two on the pop quiz she gave us. It became just like in the olden days, before Ms. Marcus said I was a poet. Back when I used to get bad grades all the time. And then, after Ms. Marcus told me I was a poet, it was like my schoolwork started getting easy. Well maybe not *easy* easy, but if I got good grades and stuff, Ms. Marcus would let me have free time to write and that made me want to get good grades. But now Ms. Cooper and her mean old words and her big old belly are leaving. We're getting a new teacher. I don't know who it's going to be, but anybody is better than her. When she told us she was leaving, I wanted to stand up in my chair and start cheering. But I knew if I did that, she'd put a mark in the book by my name and I already have enough marks in her book. I hope her book leaves with her.

I got my fingers crossed that Ms. Cooper's replacement is going to be somebody who doesn't think you need a whole published book to be a poet!

Love,

x-poet
Locomotion

Dear Lili,

A week before school started, Miss Edna got me
new notebooks and stuff. I picked a knapsack
that's blue camouflage. But when I was putting my
math book in it, Miss Edna got all choky and I
took all my books out and put them in my old
knapsack that's just green. Then I put the new one
in the far back of the closet. I don't want to be
having anything that reminds Miss Edna about
her missing her older son, Jenkins, who's over
there fighting in the war.

Clyde's in my class this year. So's Angel and
Eric. Lamont moved away. Today in the school
yard, we all stood around just looking at the other
kids playing. I was shivering because I'd only
worn my jean jacket with a T-shirt underneath
and since it's already cold, I wasn't dressed right.
Neither was Clyde—he just had a long-sleeve shirt
that was a little bit too big for him and some jeans

and just a zip-up sweatshirt. He had pulled the sleeves down over his hands and then put his hands in his pockets but he was still shivering.

Eric said, "School's stupid. Don't even know why I'm here!" He was wearing a down coat and at that moment I was wishing I was him.

Clyde told Eric he was just missing Lamont and Eric said, "I ain't thinking about no Lamont," but you could tell nobody believed him.

We all missed Lamont. The day he came up to us and told us his family was moving to Florida, none of us said anything. It was a week after the last day of school and we'd all come back to the school yard to just kind of hang and whatnot. It was hot as anything and even though Angel had brought his basketball, none of us felt like playing. That's when Lamont came running up to us all out of breath and saying that he was going to Florida. Clyde told him it was too hot to be going to Florida. Said it was about eight hundred degrees hotter than New York.

We going there to live, Lamont said. *My dad got a job. He says it's a good job. We gonna live in a house and it's gonna have a pool.* But Eric looked at him all skeptical and said, *You ain't gonna have no pool.*

Lamont grinned and took a picture out of his pocket. In the picture, there was a pretty white house and you could see the blue water from the pool just in the edge of the picture because the pool was halfway behind the house. The pool was inside the ground. I'd never in my life knew anyone who lived in a house that had a pool inside the ground. That kind of stuff only happened on TV. Eric told Lamont that he was lying. That the picture wasn't his house.

Why you gotta hate? Lamont said, and he looked all hurt, like he couldn't believe his boy wouldn't believe he was gonna live in a pretty white house with a pool. That's when Clyde told Eric that if Lamont says it's his pool then it's his pool. But Eric just looked mad.

Lamont said when they got to Florida he was going to send us a picture of his whole family swimming in that pool. Then he looked at Eric, but Eric just started walking out of the park. I said that maybe Eric was being so mean because he was getting sick again. He has sickle-cell disease and that makes him real mean sometimes. I think because it hurts his body a lot. And it's hard to be all nice and sweet when your body's hurting.

He ain't sick, Lamont said.

Nah, he ain't, Clyde said. *But I bet he's hurting real bad.*

Lamont put the picture back in his pocket and told us it wasn't like he asked his daddy to get the job. He said if it was up to him, he'd never leave Brooklyn.

We all told him that we knew that and then he gave us all *Bye, Dog* hugs. Said, *Y'all stay cool.*

We told Lamont to stay cool too and that day in the park was the last time we saw him.

That's why when Eric said that thing about everything being stupid today, I know he said it because he was missing his friend, but me and Angel and Clyde didn't say nothing else back. I mean, what could we say? Some days I just think the whole world and life and everything is stupid. And that's 'cause I be missing you.

Love,

Locomotion

```
Dear Lili,
```

Here's the scoop—I like Miss Edna and I know
you like your foster mama. So I was thinking that
it's like instead of our family getting smaller, it got
bigger, right?

When your foster mama brings you to see me
tomorrow at the agency, we're going to get to
spend the whole afternoon together and Miss
Edna said she'd take us to Junior's so we could eat
those big hamburgers and some cheesecake for
dessert. I told her you don't like cheesecake. (I bet
you thought I didn't remember, huh!)

Miss Edna was sitting there sewing a patch on
my pants where I got a hole in the knee—she likes
sewing. But she stopped sewing then and looked up
at me like it was crazy to not like cheesecake. Then
she said, *Well I guess she'll just get herself a piece of
pie or an ice cream sundae, won't she?* And I smiled
because I know how much you like ice cream.

I watched Miss Edna sew that patch on my

pants. She pulled the needle and dark blue thread real slow through the material, then stretched her arm all the way out until the thread stopped reaching. Then real slow she pushed it down into the material again. Over and over until the patch was tight against my jeans and it would take a lot of running and sliding and acting crazy to rip it off again. Miss Edna looked really peaceful. Like her mind was on something far away. Something that was making her happy—deep inside. I wondered if she was thinking about Jenkins. About the letter she'd gotten from him saying his tour was almost over and soon he'd be home from the war. I sat there wondering again why they called it a *tour* like you were going somewhere for a vacation instead of going somewhere to be in a war. I asked Miss Edna if Jenkins liked fighting.

Miss Edna smiled a little bit and shook her head. She said when Rodney and Jenkins were around my age, they'd go at it and she'd have to pull them apart. Then she laughed and said that she beat both their behinds for acting like fools when they were supposed to be brothers. Then she wasn't laughing anymore. Not even smiling. She said Jenkins never liked fighting. That in school he never got into fights and when him and

Rodney fought, Jenkins always told her Rodney
was the one who started it. But Rodney lives with
us and he's a really cool guy so I don't know. I
wasn't there. I wasn't even *born* yet.

Miss Edna stopped sewing again and told me
about the day Jenkins found out he was going
over there to the war. She said he just cried and
cried. I told her I couldn't believe he *cried*.
Miss Edna looked at me like I was crazy. Then she
told me that no matter how big you get, it's still
okay to cry if you need to because everybody's
got a right to their own tears. The thing about
Miss Edna is, she has a way of sneaking a lecture
into even the most calm conversation.

Miss Edna said Jenkins cried about having to
go fight in the war and while he was crying, she
held him real tight and told him everything was
going to be okay.

I've never met Jenkins but there's pictures of
him all over the house. The one I like the best is
the one where he's about my age and he's smiling
in one of those dumb school pictures they be
taking of us. Only thing is, he's got his fingers
sticking up behind his head, giving his own self
bunny ears. I can't believe they let him get away
with that. But every time I look at that picture, I

just start smiling and it makes me think—a kid like that would have been a good friend of mine.

I couldn't imagine that bunny-ears guy fighting in a war and told Miss Edna I didn't understand why Jenkins would even take a chance if he didn't like fighting. She told me they came to his school offering lots of money for college if he signed up for the Army Reserve and it sounded like a good idea to him. The college he wanted to go to cost so much money, Miss Edna said, that without the army, Jenkins would be paying until he was gray-headed and walking on a cane.

"My mama was saving money for me and Lili to go to college," I told her, and Miss Edna said, *It's still there.* I said, *I know. But Mama isn't.* Miss Edna didn't say anything for a little while, just put the thread between her teeth and bit it. Then tied off the end that was sticking out the patch and held the pants up. Then she folded them and held them out to me. *These go in your room, Lonnie,* she said real soft.

I got up to take them there, but Miss Edna held my wrist.

Your mama and daddy always with you, Lonnie, she told me. Then she asked me if I believed her.

I nodded, then sat back down and leaned my

head against Miss Edna's arm. I hadn't meant to get all choky. I could feel the warmth coming off her body and it felt real nice. She smelled good too—like coconut hair grease and lotion. We didn't say anything. Just sat there. Outside, I could hear kids playing freeze tag in the rain. I heard my friend Clyde say *No, y'all, I ain't it. I was standing right by base.*

Me and Miss Edna sat there talking and stuff until Rodney got home. I could hear his big feet on the stairs and him singing, *"On top of Old Smoky, all covered with rutabagas."* He always sang the same song. *"I dug a big hole and planted me some tomatas."* Then he was standing in the living room, grinning his big grin, taking off his wet jacket and chasing me into his room. Then he caught me and wrapped me up in it even though I was trying to hold on to the pants Miss Edna'd sewn and was screaming "Stop, Rodney!"

And in the living room I could hear Miss Edna saying, "You boys need to cut out that roughhousing before somebody gets hurt."

Ever since Rodney moved back to Miss Edna's house from upstate, he's been calling me his little brother. I've never been somebody's little brother before and it makes me feel good—like there's somebody else out there looking out for me just like I'm looking out for you.

Miss Edna made my favorite things—baked chicken with macaroni and cheese and corn bread and salad. I ate two big plates of food. She made a chocolate cake too. On top of it she wrote *Happy Birthday, Lonnie—Tomorrow*. And me and her and Rodney laughed about that. Then Rodney put his arm around my shoulder.

"Well, Little Brother, you almost a man now," he said.

And I smiled, thinking, *Yeah, twelve is almost a man*.

And then I said, "Yeah, Big Brother, I'm almost a man who could beat your behind!"

Rodney laughed and threw his arm around my neck. I can get out of his headlock real easy though. Then Miss Edna put the birthday candles on the cake and lit them and we stood in the small kitchen while her and Rodney sang "Happy Birthday" to me. I wish you could have been there, Lili. It still doesn't feel right to be having a birthday celebration without you around. Well, while they sang, I closed my eyes and I'm sure you know exactly what I was wishing for.

I kept my eyes closed, trying to imagine it was

you and Mama and Daddy singing, but then I got
sad because I got a hurting of missing them and I
got another hurting of missing Rodney and
Miss Edna if they weren't in my life anymore. And
the two hurtings felt like one big hurt, so I thought
about how I'm going to see you tomorrow—on my
real birthday—and some of that hurting went away.

It's real late now. Miss Edna said for me to go to
bed after I finished my letter. She likes when I
write to you. So I write you the letters and then I
put them in my drawer. I have a big collection
now. You're gonna be surprised when you get all
of them. You're gonna be reading for days. For
weeks. For years!

I'm sitting at the kitchen table. It still smells
like baked chicken and that smell is making me
hungry. After I finish this letter, maybe I'll eat the
wing off because I know Rodney and Miss Edna
saved that piece for me. Outside, the rain is
coming down and down and down.

Lili? Do you remember how much Mama loved
the rain?

Love,

Your brother forever,
Lonnie

Dear Lili,

My birthday came and the rain stopped but it was still real cold outside. I'd put on my new suit and got my hair braided real nice. I'd even put lotion on and some of Rodney's aftershave on my cheeks. It made them itch a little but I didn't care. Me and Miss Edna took the bus downtown to Remsen Street and waited for your foster mama to bring you.

Miss Edna told me I looked real nice and I told her she looked nice too. She'd worn a church dress—the yellow-and-white one that she wears a lot when it's warm outside.

Then we went back to sitting and waiting. Miss Edna and Rodney gave me a new watch for my birthday—it has a black leather strap and gold hands and numbers. I kept checking it but then Miss Edna told me to stop because her nerves were bad.

Miss Edna doesn't usually have bad nerves, just when she has to be waiting or when she's worrying about Jenkins fighting in the war. Some mornings, I see her sitting on the couch reading the newspaper and she's busy chewing on her thumbnail and doing heavy sighs. Then I know she's real worried.

I moved a little closer to Miss Edna, let my shoulder press against her arm. She put her arm around me, and then she did something she doesn't usually do—she kissed me on the top of my head.

Then my social worker, Miss Jamison, came out of her office. Her face looked like it was trying to cover up some sadness. She put her hands behind her back and pulled her pretty lips straight in a line. Her skin's real brown and sometimes when I look at her, she reminds me a little bit of Mama—the same brown skin, the same eyebrows going up when her face didn't know what else to do. Miss Jamison's eyebrows went up and she looked at me. She told me you weren't coming. Then she told me she was real sorry.

I stared at her, watching her mouth move, listening to the words coming out of it. I'd heard those same words a lot of times before, but sitting there, hearing them with all those clouds and all that grayness outside and Miss Edna's kiss still warm on my head, just made some tears push up out of me. I wiped them real fast but I know both of them saw it because Miss Edna pulled me closer and Miss Jamison looked down at the floor.

I looked up at Miss Edna and saw this look go across her face. I'd seen that same look on Mama— the time that boy in the park pushed you down and you cut your hand. I wanted Miss Edna to do some kind of magic—snatch you from wherever you were and make you appear in the foster care office. I wanted her to start fussing and making all kinds of threats about how today wasn't gonna be the day Lili didn't show up. But she didn't. Miss Edna's never yelled and she wasn't going to start yelling just because it was my birthday. Instead, she looked full at Miss Jamison and asked her if you'd be at the agency next week.

Miss Jamison said you'd be there even if she had to go get you herself.

Miss Edna nodded and said, *Well, all right then. I guess me and Lonnie will be here bright and early next Saturday.*

Later on, when we were back at Miss Edna's house, I tried to think about a million other things so I wouldn't be thinking about the one thing that was real big on my mind. I sat there not talking for a long time and then when I finally did start talking, I sounded like a really little kid. A kid who'd just dropped his ice cream cone. My voice didn't even sound like it belonged to me. I told Miss Edna that this is the first time in my whole life that I didn't get to see you on my birthday. But I couldn't say what I was really scared of—that it might not be the last.

Lili, when things don't go right in our house, Miss Edna says *Sometimes the heart breaks so hard, Lonnie.* That's what I was feeling like. Like my heart was breaking—real hard.

And then she sat down on the couch and held out her arms. And even though I know I'm way too big, I sat on her lap, put my head on her shoulder and cried and cried and cried.

Missing you,

Locomotion

Dear Lili,

It's almost October and it's raining again. The rain's been coming down since the middle of September, so people are getting their bulbs in the ground before it stops raining and the snow starts coming down. Miss Edna says when it's finally time for the sun to shine and the flowers to start showing up, it's gonna be something else. I don't know about all that. Spring seems like a long time away. But some people are digging up the little piece of ground they got going on in their front yards, so maybe Miss Edna knows what she's talking about. Her friend Miss Shore is out there every morning, down on her hands and knees, working that dirt like a crazy lady.

Today Clyde came over with his soccer ball and we were kicking it up and down the block. Clyde's feet and legs are like magic when they get around a soccer ball. He can do all kinds of tricks and was

trying to teach me how to dribble the ball from
my foot to my knee to my head then back down to
my foot again, but the ball doesn't like me like it
likes Clyde and he tried to show me about twenty
times before both of us gave up and just kicked
the ball around. Clyde kicked it real hard and it
almost went into Miss Shore's yard, and the next
thing she was out there yelling at us that if just
one of her flowers don't come up because of our
ball messing up her gardening, then we'd be fixing
her garden all summer long. *And don't think I'll be
paying you for that fixing either,* she said, all cranky
sounding. After me and Clyde moved far away
from her house and she took her crabby self back
inside, Clyde said, *She's just trying to get someone
to do her gardening for free.* We both agreed that it
wasn't going to be us because neither one of us
knows the first thing about any flowers. It doesn't
even make a little bit of sense to me that you could
put a bulb in the ground in fall and it just sits
there all winter long and then, boom, knows to
come up when the spring comes. I don't get why
the bulbs don't just freeze to death underground
in that cold frozen dirt. Clyde stopped dribbling
the ball. *Isn't it strange,* he said, *when you start*

thinking about all the hundreds of millions of things you don't know. And I said yeah. Then we just kicked the ball around without talking, letting ourselves get all wet. When Miss Edna leaned out the window and saw us all soaking wet, she asked if we knew we could catch our death of cold from the rain. And me and Clyde looked at each other and smiled. Then both of us said at the same time, *No, ma'am. We sure didn't know that.*

Love,

Locomotion

Dear Lili,

Today I sat in class watching the rain come down again. Ms. Cooper was making us write limericks but I couldn't come up with any—maybe it's because of what she said about me not being a poet and all that stuff. I wrote, *There once was a kid named Joe, Who didn't really like snow, In the springtime he was happy, In the winter he felt—* But then I knew the word I was gonna write wasn't a word Ms. Cooper would like, so I stopped writing and stared out the window. I thought about last summer when me and you went to Camp Kaufman and got to spend two weeks together like regular brothers and sisters do. I thought about how we got to eat breakfast and lunch and dinner together every day and how that one counselor would let me go say good night to you. And about how all the girls in your cabin would giggle when I came in. I know you said it was because they liked me, but I think it's just because you had a cabin full of silly girls. Then Ms. Cooper told me the poem wasn't outside the window. I think Ms. Cooper is the one that's not a poet because poetry is everywhere. I went back to writing and here's the limerick I came up with.

This morning with all of the rain

I started thinking Rain is a pain

But then out the window I saw

The summer before

And realized cold rain leads to summer again.

Love,

Lonnie
who is hoping you got to be
someplace warm and dry

Dear Lili,

Clyde came over and me and him watched
cartoons until Miss Edna told us that was enough
TV for the day. Then Clyde said, *Your mama's real
strict.* We had turned off the TV and were just
sitting on the couch. I had found this old train in
the back of my closet—I guess it had been
Jenkins's or Rodney's when they were little kids.
Miss Edna said it was okay to play with. I had the
caboose in my hand, just kind of running it back
and forth along the couch arm. Clyde had the
other parts of it and he started running them
along the back of the couch, then over the
window, making some kind of fake train noise. At
least, that's what I guess it was supposed to be. I
told Clyde for the hundred millionth time that
Miss Edna wasn't my real mama. Then Clyde
stopped playing with the train and just sat there
looking at me. He was wearing a Mets shirt and

some real old-looking jeans. I didn't care about the old jeans, just was glad he was wearing that Mets shirt since that's my favorite team. I told him again that the reason I called her Miss Edna was because she was only a foster mama. Sometimes it was like he had amnesia or something. I didn't say that part but I was thinking it real hard. Clyde just looked at me and asked if Miss Edna told me what I could be doing and what I couldn't be doing. I said yeah and then Clyde said, *She hug you sometimes?* I nodded then. I was embarrassed because once Clyde saw Miss Edna give me a big hug right outside where all my friends was watching. She was real happy because she'd gotten a letter from Jenkins saying he was okay. So she just started dancing around and hugging me like a crazy lady. Then Clyde said, *You got another mama?* And even though he's my best friend, I wanted to hit him hard. He knew the answer to that question. *You know my mama died, man!* I was starting to get mad. Clyde put his hand on my shoulder and told me that all he was trying to say was that Miss Edna was my mama now and I could call her whatever I wanted to be calling her but she was my for-real mama.

I looked at Clyde for a long time but didn't say anything to him. He looked at me right back. He kept his hand on my shoulder and kept his voice real soft. *There's all kinds of mamas,* he said. Then he told me that when he lived down south, his grandmamma was his mama and kids used to always ask him how come his mama is so old and he said he told them that she was old because she was old. When I asked Clyde how come his grandma didn't come to New York with him, he took his hand off my shoulder and looked down at his fingers. Then he told me she died and that's why his mama brought him and his sister to New York.

Clyde looked at me again. When Miss Edna first met him, she said, "Well you must have the prettiest eyes of any boy I've ever seen in my life!" And Clyde had grinned. I guess he had okay eyes if you like eyes. I guess Miss Edna likes eyes because she tells me mine are nice too.

Clyde said his mama had people here in Brooklyn and that's who him and his sister stay with but his mama stays in the Bronx. Miss Edna came in and brought us some peanut butter crackers and we both said thank you. When she went out of the room again, I asked Clyde how come his mama didn't live with them.

"She just don't," Clyde said. "But that's okay. Me and my sister like my aunt a whole lot. She's like a new mama to us. She's real kind." When he said the word *kind,* it sounded real down south— taking a long time to disappear the way those down-south words be doing.

I told Clyde his aunt was nice. It's true. Whenever I went to Clyde's apartment, his aunt would give us fruit snacks and gum. Or Ritz crackers with peanut butter on them. Good stuff like that.

"Yeah," Clyde said. Then he went back to running the train track and engine along the back of the couch. I crashed into it with my train car and we kept doing that, just running the trains and crashing them. Running the trains and crashing them.

Until Miss Edna said it was dinnertime.

Love,

Locomotion

Dear Lili,

Today we got a new teacher and she's not even a little bit like Ms. Cooper. The first thing she said when she called on me was *I heard lots about you. Aren't you the young man who likes writing poetry?* And I had to smile real big. I asked her if Ms. Cooper told her that and she said no—that she was good friends with Lucy Marcus. (I didn't even know that was Ms. Marcus's first name!) She said all summer long, Ms. Marcus had talked about Lonnie Collins Motion—how people should keep an eye out for me. The other kids in the class started making jealous sounds but I didn't care. I'd gone a whole three months with that old Ms. Cooper and now here was this new teacher. I sat up real straight in my chair. Angel said, "It's true, that boy can write!" and then some other kids agreed with him. Maybe they were just trying to get on her good side but I didn't care. I'm going to try to do real good in all my other subjects for the rest of the year—not just in writing.

Love,

Locomotion

Dear Lili,

I can't write a real lot tonight. We got news that
Jenkins is missing from the war. Something bad
happened and nobody knows where he's at.
Miss Edna's been praying all day and Rodney's
been on the phone trying to get some information.
Miss Edna sat down hard on the couch and let
out deep, shaky breaths. Rodney sat down
beside her and put his arm around her shoulder.
He kept saying, *It's gonna be all right, Mama.
Everything's gonna be all right.* I said that maybe
we should turn on the news and Rodney thought
that was a good idea. I turned on the television
and sat down on the other side of Miss Edna and
held her hand. She kept saying over and over—
Lord, please bring my baby back home. We
watched the CNN channel that has news all the
time. The newscaster lady kept talking about
insurgents and a car bomb and missing soldiers. I

waited to see Jenkins's face on the screen. For
some reason, I thought I'd see him there smiling
and holding those rabbit ears up behind
someone's head—but it didn't happen. Miss Edna
finally got up and went into her room. I made me
and Rodney some peanut butter sandwiches and
we turned the news off and just sat there for a
while, chewing and not saying nothing. Rodney
said that his mama was probably in her room
praying and I asked what he thought we should
be praying for.

"Peace, man," he said. "Pray for peace."

I'd almost finished my sandwich but Rodney
still had a whole half of his to go. I asked him,
didn't he want to pray for Jenkins being okay?
Because that's what I was thinking about praying
for. Rodney was about to put some sandwich in
his mouth, but he put it back down on his plate.
We were sitting on the couch kind of facing each
other and he leaned a little bit closer to me.

"The way I see it," he said. "You pray for
peace, all the rest of the stuff comes. If there
was peace, nobody would be getting hurt or
killed or jacked up in a war, right?"

I nodded.

"Peace covers everything, Little Brother. *Everything.*"

So now I'm in my room and the lamp is on so that I can finish writing you this letter. From now on, I'm gonna be doing everything about peace, Lili. I'm going to be praying for it and thinking about it and trying to make it a part of every single thing.

Peace, Lili.

Love, your brother forever, Lonnie

Dear Lili,

Today my new teacher said something that got me
thinking. She said every day you should try to
write or think about or talk about *one true thing*.
Her name's Miss Alina and that's her first name.
She said we don't have to even use the "Ms." if
we don't want to. That we could just call her
Alina. Clyde didn't like that one bit. *It's not
respectful,* he said, and some of the new kids who
didn't know Clyde before laughed at him because
he still has that accent and all. But Clyde—it's
like he doesn't even hear when people are
laughing at him. It's like there's this shield around
him and the laughter doesn't even get inside him.
Even if somebody just laughed a tiny bit at
something I said, I'd feel real bad about it. I guess
that's why I like Clyde—'cause he's the opposite of
me in a lot of ways. He's real smart and I'm not
real smart. He talks country and I hardly

remember down south since it's been such a long time since we been there. He's tall—like if he really wanted to, he could play pro ball and as you know, I'm not real tall (yet), so even though I'd love to play some pro ball one day, I can't be seriously believing it the way Clyde can because he's already half there—I mean, like with his height but not with his game. Anyway, me and Clyde are real good friends now, so when the kids started laughing about the way he talks, I turned around in my seat and gave a mean stare to the ones I knew was laughing. Most kids don't mess with me. Not because they real scared of me. I know they don't mess with me because they know about Mama and Daddy and how they died and all. Sometimes I see the old ones whispering to the new ones and then the new ones look at me all pitiful. And that's when I wish I had more of Clyde in me—so I could make that invisible shield and their pitiful looks couldn't get through.

"You a grown person," Clyde said to the teacher. "It's respectful to call grown people by Mr. or Miss or Mrs."

Miss Alina—*Alina*—smiled. I didn't know any grown-ups I called by their first name and I liked the idea of it, so I wanted Clyde to not be reminding her that that's something kids aren't supposed to do.

Miss Alina is not real tall and she's brown like Mama. Her hair is always in braids and then she pulls the braids back in a ponytail. And guess what, Lili. Her eyebrow is pierced and there's a little gold ring coming out of it. The first day she came to our class, LaTenya asked her, *Did that hurt?* Miss Alina touched her eyebrow ring-thingie and smiled and told us that it hurt when she first got it done but now she doesn't even know it's there most of the time. LaTenya wanted to know how she plucked her eyebrows. Alina just smiled and said she didn't. Then LaTenya looked all confused because she thought all grown-up ladies plucked their eyebrows. And Alina said, *Depends on the grown-up lady. And personally, I like bushy eyebrows.* LaTenya ran her fingers over her own eyebrows and stared at Alina with all this . . . *wonder.*

I snuck my hand up and touched my own eyebrows. They're *kinda* bushy, right? I still call her Miss Alina to her face, but when I'm thinking about her after school and stuff, I think of her as

Alina. That's the *one true thing* for today, Lili.
Mama didn't pluck her eyebrows and Alina
doesn't pluck hers. Grown-ups come in all kinds
of ways.

One other true thing—Peace.

Lonnie

Dear Lili,

It's Saturday. I'm supposed to be seeing you but
nobody, even me, wants to leave the house in case
the phone rings. I called Miss Jamison myself to
say I wasn't coming. Later on, I'm gonna call you
at your foster mama's house, okay? But right now,
I'm just sitting in my room and writing.
Sometimes, when I'm writing—even if it's not
something like poetry or a comic-strip story, even
if it's a letter to you—it makes me feel better
inside. It's makes things more . . . more . . . *clear.*

They found Jenkins last night. He's still alive
but he's not good. Rodney said I shouldn't tell you
too much because it would just make you have
bad dreams at night.

Peace, Lili.

Locomotion

Dear Lili,

I'm sitting on my bed. It's real gray out and
raining a little bit. I can hear Miss Edna in her
room. Just crying and crying. Right on the
table beside me is the picture of Jenkins with
those fingers behind his head. I look at it and
try to smile with him being so goofy and all.
But no smile comes out of me. Just some of
Miss Edna's tears.

Crazy crying for somebody you never met,
right? But I guess since I've been living with
Miss Edna for two years now and I've been
knowing Rodney and hearing about Jenkins and
seeing his pictures since day one, it's kind of like
he's already a brother to me. A faraway brother.

Lili, I was thinking. This war's been going on a
real long time. Eric said when he grows up he's
going to join the army. Then Clyde looked at him
real crazy and told him that he wasn't going to

have to join because they were going to *draft* him. Even Eric got quiet. He didn't even make fun of the way Clyde talks, just shrugged and kept staring out at the school yard. But Angel said Clyde was wrong—that you have to go to a war on your own, that they can't be making you go. But Clyde just shook his head and looked at all of us like we were crazy. Clyde moved from down south when we were all in the fifth grade last year. At first everybody thought he was kind of slow but it was just the way he talked. Turned out, Clyde was smarter than most of us. Once we all figured that out, we started paying more attention to him and not making fun of him and stuff. Before Clyde came, I hadn't really had a best friend—just the guys I hung out with all the time. But now it's different. A best friend is a cool thing to have. "Y'all don't get it," Clyde said, looking around at each of us. "They almost all run out of guys who *want* to be going to fight in some war."

Clyde was wearing jeans that looked real old. All his clothes looked like they'd been worn by a hundred other boys before they got to him. Clyde folded his arms and leaned back against the fence. He told us that once the guys that *want* to be fighting get all used up, they're going to come after the ones that *don't* want to be fighting. He said, *It's called a draft, fools.*

Eric said, *What you talking about, son? Used up. You act like we talking about toilet paper.*

We all laughed. Except Clyde. He looked like he felt sorry for us. He let us go on laughing a little while, then he started talking again, his voice real low. *Used up. Broke down. Shot up. Dead. That's the used up I'm talking about.* I thought about Jenkins. I told them they found him and everybody wanted to know if he was still alive. I said yeah and then I told them the other stuff. Clyde said it's messed up. He said there ain't one person over there who don't have a nice heart. I thought about Jenkins's heart. If it was anything like Rodney's and Miss Edna's, then it was real nice.

"I ain't going out like that," Eric said. "No way, son."

Angel nodded but he didn't say anything. He put his hand in his pocket and took out a Hershey bar, then broke it in four pieces and gave us each some. Then he broke off a little bit of his piece and dropped it on the ground.

"For Lonnie's brother Jenkins," Angel said. "And for the guys that ain't here no more." We all did the same thing. Even Eric said, *For the brothers that are gone.*

Peace, Lili. Pray for Peace.

Locomotion

Dear Lili,

The one true thing for today—sometimes people
say something about you and no matter how hard
you try not to believe it, you still do. Every time
I tried to write a poem about Jenkins today,
Ms. Cooper's voice was in my head telling me I
wasn't a real poet. So the poem never came.

Love,

Lonnie

Dear Lili,

I'm glad you got a hundred percent on your math
test. It's good to know *somebody* in our family can
do math. Miss Edna said your foster mama said
you're one of the smartest kids she's ever met in her
life. Said everybody at church always talking about
what a smart and pretty girl you are. Even though I
wish I had some of your smartness, I still feel real
proud to know you're doing so good in school.
Wish I could say the same for me! But today after
school while I was trying to do my science
homework, Rodney came into the kitchen and sat
down across from me. He said, *You know I'm gonna
be a teacher one day, so why don't you let me help you
with that, Li'l Brother?* I looked at him and said, *Your
mama says you didn't do good in school so—a: how
you gonna be a teacher and b: how you gonna help me?*
Rodney just threw his head back and laughed. He
really does have the best laugh of anybody. Then he

grabbed my notebook from me and looked at my work. *This stuff's easy,* he said. *You just using the wrong part of your brain. You trying to think all deep about something that's really simple.* Then real carefully he explained to me about photosynthesis. He said it's like plants breathing—that just like we breathe in oxygen and breathe out carbon dioxide, plants take in carbon dioxide and then produce oxygen through their leaves. Then real slow, Rodney explained all about carbohydrates and chlorophyll and even talked about how the sun worked. We sat at that table for a whole hour, but it felt like only a little bit of time had passed. Then Rodney asked me to explain parts back to him and his smile got so big, I knew I was telling it right! *You got a brain, Li'l Brother,* he said to me. I said— *Nah, man. You're the one with the brain. I thought you didn't like school and stuff though.* Rodney took a pack of gum out of his pocket and gave me a piece. Then we both just sat there chewing for a minute. *When I was living upstate, I had all this time to think about things. My mind's always going and going. Been like that since I was a little kid. But it wasn't going like teachers wanted it to be so they always tried to get me to do things different.* Rodney looked at me and smiled. *When I was a kid and even when I was a teenager, I always thought it was me. But when I got older, I started realizing that I just got stuck with some lame teachers,* he said. *And they made me think I wasn't a good student, so I just wasn't.* I thought about Ms. Cooper. *Upstate, I just got mad about it. I was mad somebody had made me feel stupid for so much of my life.* I asked him if that's when he decided he wanted to be a teacher and he said yeah. *It would be cool,* Rodney said, *to make some of those kids who think they're not smart suddenly see how smart they really are.* Then he looked at me and winked. I thought about Ms. Cooper again. And then I thought about Ms. Marcus, my teacher from last year who said I was a good poet. I sure did miss her. I wanted to tell Rodney that I thought he was going to be a real good teacher, but I didn't say anything. We just sat there chewing our gum. When I see you, Lili, I'm gonna explain this photosynthesis thing to you.

Peace,

Locomotion

Dear Lili,

You make me laugh. When I told you about Miss Alina today and you asked me if I was in love with her, I had to crack up because only you would say something that crazy. You can't fall in love with your teacher, girl. Plus, Miss Alina is like twenty years older than me! I could tell you didn't believe me because you started doing that *mmm-hmmm* thing Mama used to do when she knew I was lying and I could imagine you standing in your foster mama's kitchen with the phone to your ear and your lips pulled to the side, rolling your eyes just like Mama would. Some days you look so much like Mama and you act so much like Mama, I feel like I'm *your* child. Now I'm sitting here writing and all I can remember is you saying "Sounds like you in love, Big Brother" in that know-it-all voice you're starting to have all the time these days.

It's strange watching you grow up, Lili. You used to be so tiny. I'd sit at the window and hold you in my arms and we'd both look out at our old block. Sometimes you'd jump for no reason like you'd heard a loud noise or something and I'd have to grab you real fast before you fell off my lap. And sometimes you'd just start laughing at something you saw out the window, but I could never see the thing that was so funny to you. And now you're getting tall and have your ears pierced and your nails polished and laugh like Mama used to laugh and be figuring I'm lying through the phone lines.

It's strange growing up away from you like this. But each day, it seems to get a little bit more familiar.

Love,

Locomotion

Dear Lili,

Today in class, LaTenya passed me a note that said, *Dear Lonnie. Remember last year when we used to hang out sometimes? LaTenya.* Lili, here's the one true thing for today—I think LaTenya is the prettiest girl in the whole sixth-grade class. Sometimes, when I see her with her friends and she's smiling, my whole body feels like it's lifting right up into the sky to hang out with the pigeons. Isn't that crazy? I can't tell anybody that because my boys would just laugh at me. But when I got that note from LaTenya, I got that body-lifting feeling and my hand was shaking when I wrote her back. I wrote, *Yeah, I remember.* Then at lunchtime, she was standing by the fence all by herself and I went over to her and we just started talking about stuff. She said her parents were taking them all to Puerto Rico for Christmas and I asked her why were they going to Puerto Rico since they weren't Puerto

Rican. LaTenya smiled that pretty smile of hers and said, *We're going for a vacation, Lo. Don't you ever go on vacation?* I felt kind of bad then because it's been a real long time since I been on a vacation. I remember the time we all went to Disneyland and you were too small for most of the rides. I got on a whole bunch without you but you didn't cry. You just kept calling my name every time the ride came by you. And it was real sunny in Disneyland and Mama and Daddy bought us every single thing we asked for. I told LaTenya about that time and she said she always wanted to go to Disneyland but both her sisters wanted to go to Puerto Rico and in their house majority rules. We talked until the bell rang and as I was walking inside, Clyde ran up on me and looked at me and looked at LaTenya, then nodded real slow like he understood everything in the world. And you know what? Sometimes I think my boy does.

Peace, Lili.

Locomotion

Dear Lili,

Here's the poem I wrote today.

Sometimes,

You can think

About life

And everything that makes your life

Your life.

Today I am thinking about living

In Brooklyn

On Gates Avenue, top floor.

And about people who can't see the sky

From their windows.

And I'm thinking about LaTenya

Maybe sitting in her own window

And watching a whole different world go by.

I don't know if it makes any sense. It just came to me fast, so I wrote it down. I hope you like it. See you the day after tomorrow.

Peace,

Lonnie

Dear Lili,

Today when you ran into my arms, you almost
knocked me over, girl! When did you do all that
growing?

"Lonnie!"

And when did your foster mama straighten
your hair? And how come it hangs all the way
down your back—like . . . guess?

Yup. Like Mama. She would wear those braids
all the time and then come Saturday night, they
would get us that mean babysitter—what was her
name? I'll think of it. Well, they'd get all dressed
up and Mama would have gotten her hair done—
all straightened out and hanging just like yours.
I almost fell over when I saw you, girl! Well,
it didn't help that you were almost knocking
me over.

"Lonnie! I haven't seen you in forever!"

And there you were, with your orange dress on

and your white tights and pretty hair. And your face all smiling and shiny, just staring at me like you couldn't believe your eyes.

And then you were throwing your arms around my neck all over again and I thought, *This girl ain't never gonna let go.*

But then you did. And I love how we stood there, grinning like crazy. I put my arm around your shoulder and we walked over to where Miss Edna and your foster mama couldn't be— that private area where they can see us but they can't really hear what we're saying. I told you to sit down and you said **You** *sit down!* in that new grown-up way you have of talking now. So we both sat down at the same time in those plastic chairs.

When you said to me, "You always look so nice and everything," and touched my braids, seemed like you be forgetting that I'm the older kid in this family! Then you said, *Mama says you can come to church with us next week.* I sat there a long time, thinking maybe I didn't hear what I thought I heard. That's why I asked *What'd you just call her?* because I couldn't believe it. Your eyes got real wide and you looked confused. Then you looked scared because maybe something in my face was mad. I didn't mean for it to be. But you know me better than anybody and you can see things that other people can't see. Like the mad real deep down. And the sadness I be trying to not let get to me.

"Mama," you finally said. Real soft. "I called her Mama."

I felt like something was breaking inside of me. I felt like I could hear our own true Mama looking down at us and biting her lip to keep tears from coming.

"She's not your mama, Lili," I whispered. I looked over to where Miss Edna and your foster mama were. They were sitting in the waiting area but they weren't sitting together. Miss Edna was reading a magazine and your foster mama was reading her Bible. Then Miss Edna leaned over and said something to your foster mama and she nodded and said something back. Real soft, you told me you knew that. The room was hot. The agency had the heat going and the windows had steam on them. Somewhere I could even hear some steam coming out of a radiator. I looked around for the sound but couldn't find it. I couldn't look right at you for a while. I heard Miss Edna laugh and looked back over. She'd closed her magazine and was steady talking to your foster mama.

"We got a Mama, Lili."

"That Mama's in heaven," you said. "I want a mama right here, Lonnie."

I thought about what Clyde had said about Miss Edna being my mama. Then you came over and hugged me.

"That's why I want you to be the rememberer," you said. "I want the Mama I used to have and the Mama I got now. I don't want to not have one or not have the other."

Your arms were still around my shoulder and I reached up and touched your hand. It was soft. Your nails had pink polish on them. Your fingers are long and brown—not like Mama's—like Daddy's. He always said I got Mama's hands and you got his hands.

"Mama used to read us a book called *Stevie*," I said. "It was about this little boy and he came to live with this other little boy whose name was Robert. And Robert was older and he didn't like Stevie because his mama paid all kinds of attention to Stevie."

That's when you sat down again and folded your hands. You looked right at me. Listening. Waiting to hear more. You smiled and your eyes got a kind of faraway look—like you were right back there with our real mama, hearing the story.

"So then Robert was always wishing Stevie's mama would come and take him home."

"And then she did one day, right?"

I nodded.

"I kinda remember it, Lonnie. The big kid . . . Robert? Well, he was sad when Stevie went away, right?"

I said yeah.

"If Mama and Daddy came back to life and came and got me from my new mama, I'd be sad too."

I didn't say anything. It was turning into a kinda sad visit.

"Wouldn't you?"

"Yeah," I said. "I guess."

But, Lili—I wasn't telling the whole truth. I'd be a lot sad if I had to move away from Miss Edna and my brothers.

'Cause—yeah, I guess they are my brothers now, right?

And you know something—I think Mama and
Daddy would like them. I think they just want to
make sure you and me are happy. And home safe.

I love you, Lili.

Your brother always.

Peace,
Lonnie

Dear Lili,

Today after school me and Angel and Clyde
and Eric were playing ball in the freezing cold and
Eric started saying he had a dream about Lamont
and in the dream, Lamont was in his warm
backyard in his big swimming pool. We all started
talking about how lucky Lamont was to not have
to be in New York City in the wintertime. I was so
cold, my fingers were hurting, and Clyde couldn't
hardly talk because he was shivering so much.
Eric kept running up to the basket trying to do
layups (and missing) but the whole time he was
talking about Lamont and the stuff they used to
do together. He said one time him and Lamont
walked all the way from Brooklyn to Harlem. *It
took us from the morning to the afternoon,* he said.
*And by the time we got to One Two Five Street, our
dogs was tired!* Then Eric got this grin on his face
and said it was real nice to just be walking with

your friend and talking junk. We all said yeah
because none of us had ever heard Eric talk that
much about anything and see him be so happy
with a memory. Angel said when the weather
wasn't so cold anymore we should all walk to
Harlem in memory of Lamont and his crazy self.
Then snow started coming down—first just a few
flakes, then a whole lot, and we just stopped
playing ball and stood there looking up at the sky.
I think we were all thinking about Lamont. Maybe
he was sitting in his pool with a soda in his hand,
staring up at his own Florida sky and
remembering us.

Stay warm, Baby Sis.

Locomotion

Dear Lili,

It's dark outside. I went up on the roof and was sitting there looking at the stars. And I was talking to Mama and Daddy. You know how a long time ago, I told you that maybe that's what they were now—stars? I told you that because you were just a little kid then and I wanted you to believe that Mama and Daddy was still with us. But then, guess what? Here's the one true thing for today: A part of me started to believe it too and so I go up on the roof some nights and just stare up at the stars and whisper things that I'm thinking about and that I'm hoping.

Sometimes the stars flicker.

Like tonight—a little bit of light was coming off of one and then a little bit of light started coming off another one and then everywhere I looked, it seemed like the stars got that twinkling and flickering going on. You know what, Lili? I think they're happy. I think Mama and Daddy are together up in that sky and I think they be looking down at us all the time. I think they know you got those new teeth you showed me last time I saw you, and I think they know about you loving the color yellow, and about the war, and me loving poetry and Peace and everything. I think when people have to leave you on Earth, they don't really be leaving you a hundred percent. I think some little part of them is always right here with us . . .

Forever.

Peace,
Lonnie

Dear Lili,

We still haven't gotten news about when Jenkins is coming home. Miss Edna cries and cries. Last night when I was talking to Mama and Daddy, I told them about everything that's going on and stuff. And I asked them to send Jenkins home to us soon.

I know you go to church with your foster mama every Sunday. And I know you think I should be praying to God for Jenkins, so that's what I'm doing. And I'm asking everybody else to hope and pray real hard too. I figure you can't have too much hope and you can't do too much begging if you want something real bad, right? I know you love God and I know I love you and I love all the things you love (except pink and playing baby with dolls!). But Lili? Sometimes I'm sitting on that roof and it's like Mama's sitting on one side of me and Daddy's sitting on the other and the both of them's got their arms around my shoulders and we're all staring up at the stars and smiling.

And you know something else? You're there, Little Sister. You're sitting on Mama's lap and your skinny little arm is pointing up at the stars. Some nights, I figure you're looking at Orion's belt—that's the three stars just in this straight line. And some nights you're looking at the Big Dipper and you're telling Mama you want some soup!

That's the thing about people dying, Lili. You have all these frozen memories in your head and the longer they stay dead, the more your memory gets all gray—like I don't know if we ever really all sat together up on a roof somewhere or not. I just know when I'm sitting there by myself, a part of me just gets all these pictures in my head—like a movie or something. And you know what, Lili? Me and you and Mama and Daddy are the stars of that movie.

We're the stars, Lili. We're the heroes of the whole story. *The Motion Family*—a major motion picture. Can you even imagine?

Tonight I went back up on the roof and said

that out loud. I whispered, *We're the stars!* And then the stars twinkled and twinkled. That made me smile, Lili. And the smile felt better than anything.

```
Peace,
Lonnie
```

Dear Lili,

I got up this morning and there wasn't anything
smelling like breakfast. Usually Miss Edna makes
me eggs or pancakes or, if it's Saturday, she makes
French toast. It's real easy to make—you just mix
eggs and milk and some cinnamon and vanilla.
Then you pour it on a plate and dip pieces of
bread in that. Then you put the pieces of bread in
a frying pan that butter's melting in. You cook it
until it's nice and brown, then you turn it over.
But guess what—there's a secret to making French
toast. You gotta poke it with a fork while it's
cooking. I don't know why. Miss Edna just does
that. She says her mama did it.

Miss Edna's mama died a long time ago.

Our mama and daddy died when I was seven
and you were four. And now Jenkins isn't waking
up. Seems like every time life starts straightening
itself all out, something's gotta go and happen.

I took a shower and put on my clothes. The
whole house was quiet. But while I was sitting in
the kitchen, eating a bowl of cereal without any
milk in it, Rodney came in. He was rubbing his
eye with one hand and scratching his shoulder
with the other. I almost smiled at that. He said,
Hey, Little Brother, and I said *Hey, yourself* and
asked him if he was okay. He say yeah and asked
me if I was okay. I told him I was all right.

Rodney sat down across from me and took
a Cheerio out of my bowl. When you looked
at him real good, all you saw was Miss Edna—
Miss Edna's mouth, Miss Edna's black eyebrows.
Miss Edna's teeth with the space between the two
front ones.

"You need some milk with that," he said. I told
him we didn't have any left and Rodney let out a
deep breath and leaned back. He wasn't wearing a
shirt, so I got a good look at all the muscles all over
his body. Then I sat up a little straighter trying to
stick my chest out. But I don't really have muscles
yet. Just skinniness. Milk's supposed to help you
build muscles and stuff. Usually, Miss Edna
remembers to buy more when it's running out.

"Miss Edna sleeping?"

"Yeah. I hope Jenkins wakes up because I don't know what Mama . . ." He stopped talking and looked down at his hands. "I just hope he's all right, Little Brother."

Rodney got up and got himself a glass of water. He stood in the kitchen watching me eat my cereal. Then he asked me if I was going to school and I nodded. He stood there another minute.

"How's school, Lo?"

I told him I liked it okay. That it was a little bit better now that Miss Alina was our teacher.

Rodney said that Jenkins really liked school when he was my age. Said Jenkins couldn't understand why Rodney didn't like school. *When we was little,* Rodney said, *he'd be telling me how much he loved going to school because it was filling his head with all this new stuff and that new stuff was real exciting for him.* Rodney looked at me, then he looked down at the floor.

I told Rodney that I guess I'm a little bit like him and a little bit like Jenkins and that made him smile.

"How you figure?"

"Because I like school, you know, but I don't be understanding a lot of stuff and when I do understand it, it's like I got a new room in my brain that's all filled with that stuff."

Rodney's smile got a little bigger.

I told Rodney that I bet Jenkins was gonna wake up. Wake up and come home. Rodney said, *Thanks, Lo,* but his voice broke all up when he said it.

Then he sniffed and left the kitchen. A minute later, I heard the door to his room close.

I got up and rinsed out my bowl. Then I took some money from the jar over the sink.

Miss Edna likes milk in her coffee. I'd make sure that tomorrow there was some in the fridge for her.

Tonight, I'm thinking about Peace, Lili. I'm thinking about Peace real hard because I don't want to get drafted and I don't want more people to get used up. I close my eyes and I see the peace sign. I draw peace signs on my notebook. I try to picture everybody putting down their weapons and no more wars anywhere.

Peace,

Lonnie

Dear Lili,

It was real nice to go to church with you today. I liked when your foster mama hugged me and told me she was glad I came. Maybe she was just doing it because the church ladies were watching. But it doesn't matter. A hug's a hug, right? And it seems like she smiles at me more and more these days, so maybe the hug really did come from her heart. When the choir started singing that song about hope being everywhere and when they started swaying from side to side in those red robes, it just looked like one big blanket of red moving back and forth, all slow and peaceful. And I liked when you went up there and you started singing with them and your voice was so beautiful, Lili. I can't believe they let you sing that whole part all by yourself. I snuck a look over at your foster mama and she looked real proud. Like you were her true-blue child and you had been sent down from the heaven y'all were singing about just to be with her. But my favorite part was when you came back down the aisle and you were smiling and looking at me. And when you sat down between me and your foster mama, then leaned over and whispered, *I sang really good because I knew you were listening.*

And I was. I really, truly was. You know what? There's peace in your music, Lili. When the organ guy was playing real soft and the choir was just swaying and humming and that beautiful light was coming into the church from the yellow windows, I just sat there smiling because it was like somebody had floated over and pulled warm covers over me.

Peace and Music,

Lonnie

Dear Lili,

Guess what? Jenkins woke up today. And the first thing he did was ask for his mama. That's what they told Miss Edna when they called. She cried and cried. But she kept saying *Don't worry, y'all. These are happy tears.* Strange how crying can be happy crying. But I could tell Miss Edna was telling the truth because she was smiling the whole time. When she hung up the phone, she hugged me and Rodney real hard. Then she went in her room, got on her knees and thanked God and Jesus and Jenkins's guardian angel.

    Amen, Miss Edna said.

    Amen.

    Peace, Lili. Keep praying for Peace. There's still a whole lot of guys over there.

Love,

Locomotion

Dear Lili,

One of Jenkins's legs is missing. He's coming home
in a month.

Love and Peace,

Locomotion

Dear Lili,

It's raining again. But it's that crazy kind of rain
with the sun shining behind it. When I went
outside this morning, Clyde was sitting on our
stoop.

I been waiting in this rain for you, he said. He
had his basketball and his hoodie pulled over his
head. The ball was so wet, it was shining.

I asked Clyde how come he didn't ring my bell.

'Cause I like sitting in the rain, he said. *And I
knew that you'd come outside when it was time.*

I said when it was time for what and Clyde said
back, *Just when it was time for you to be outside.*

We played some taps and then we just dribbled
the ball back and forth for a while. Clyde's a real
good dribbler and I tried to watch him to see if I
could learn something. But he's got fast hands, so
the ball was just a blur. I told him Jenkins was
coming home and Clyde kept dribbling but it

slowed way down. He didn't say anything for a while, then he said, *That's good, Lo.* And he just kept on dribbling, like his mind was real far away. Then Clyde asked me if I was scared of meeting Jenkins. I said no and he looked at me and said, *You sure?* Then I just shrugged because I was a little bit scared.

When Jenkins comes home, things are probably going to be real different. Miss Edna's house isn't that big and my room used to be Rodney's room, so now Rodney's in Jenkins's room. Miss Edna has one more room next to the kitchen that she keeps all kinds of stuff in and she's been throwing stuff out and moving it to her room and some into the living room closet. She says eventually we're going to have to move to a building with an elevator, but until we can, that's going to be Jenkins's new room. I don't know how much he's going to like being kicked out of his old room. Miss Edna says he'll be glad because there's a window in his new room and he used to complain when he was a kid that it wasn't fair that he didn't have a room with a window. Even though Miss Edna's been my foster mama for a long time and I've been living here for all these

years, it's hard not to feel like I'm putting
people out.

So yeah, I am a little bit scared. I guess Clyde
could tell because he said, *It's gonna be all right,
man. Just gonna take some time and all.* Then he
told me that whenever his mama decides to come
live with them again, it's always a whole lot of
changing going on—first him and his sister have
to get used to her being there. He said his sister
gets used to it real fast since she's only nine and
she starts hugging his mama and kissing her and
staying real close to her, hugging her leg or arm or
neck like the scariest thing in the world is that
she's not going to be touching her mama.

Clyde said he just keeps an eye on his mama
and tries to figure out when she's going to leave
again so that he can know when to get ready to
take care of his sister, because she gets real sad.
Clyde said you get used to people coming and
going. We talked a long time—just throwing the
ball back and forth and me practicing my
dribbling. I told him that sometimes I think I'm
going to see Mama and Daddy coming around the
corner, laughing and holding hands. Then me and
you go running up to them and you jump up in

Daddy's arms. Clyde thought that was a good
memory to have in my head. We played some more
taps, then I asked him if he wanted to go to the
park to shoot some hoops and Clyde said he
needed to get home to make his sister some dinner
because his aunt was at work. Then I went on
inside and did my homework. That was mostly
what the day was.

Peace, Lili.

Locomotion

Dear Lili,

Today me and Miss Edna did grocery shopping.
We took the bus over to Vanderbilt Avenue
because that's where there's the good store that has
cheaper prices. At least, that's what Miss Edna
says. She checks the prices of everything and if
something costs too much, she frowns and puts it
back on the shelf. I know we're not rich because
of a lot of reasons, but mostly when I see Miss
Edna putting stuff back or counting the money in
her wallet or at night sometimes when she's paying
bills—that's when I really know. Sometimes she'll
say to me, *Lonnie, turn off that light if you're not
using it. You act like we own the electric company.*
Once I asked her if we were real poor and she
rubbed her hand over my head and said, *You too
young to be worrying about money. We'll always get
by.* Then she said something that made me real
happy, Lili. She said, *And you'll always have
everything you need.* I didn't mind about not having

everything I wanted, because I know sometimes I want stuff that I don't really need. But when Miss Edna said that, it made me believe that I'd always have food and warm clothes and her and you.

On the way home, me and Miss Edna were each carrying two bags and I even had some groceries in my knapsack. There was a man sitting on the corner in a wheelchair and one of his legs was missing. I got scared and dropped one of the bags and some of the cans in it rolled out. I kept telling Miss Edna I was sorry and she kept saying, *Don't worry, Lonnie. Nothing broke.* The man in the wheelchair said he wished he could help us and I saw Miss Edna get kinda teary, but she just smiled at him and told him to stay blessed. He said, *Same to you.*

All the way home on the bus, me and Miss Edna didn't say anything to each other. But after we got home and put the groceries away, we each went into our rooms and stayed there mostly the whole afternoon.

Peace, Lili.

Locomotion

Dear Lili,

Outside, the snow is coming down *crazy*. There's
already a whole lot of it on the ground and the
branches on that big tree down the block look like
they're gonna fall right off with all that snow on
them. Me and Clyde had a snowball fight on the
way home from school and I threw one that got him
right in the back of the head. He was real mad for a
minute but then he just started laughing. He said—
Man, you sure can throw! Then he snuck one up on
me—a big one that he had been hiding behind his
back. He smushed it down my back. It was
freezing! Man, that snowball fight was real fun. But
then Miss Shore saw us throwing all that snow
around and came outside with two shovels. She told
us that since we liked the snow so much, we could
get busy getting it out from in front of her house,
then we could see if any other *seniors* was needing
someone to shovel for them. That's what she calls
old people—*seniors*. Like they're about to graduate
from high school or something. Miss Shore told us

not to shovel too deep where her dirt was because of those bulbs she'd put in the ground. She said if even a single one of her bulbs didn't come up, she'd have us working all spring to fix her garden. Man—that is one cranky lady. I can't believe her garden looks so nice in the spring with all that evil she got in her. Clyde was supposed to come over to hang and do homework but we ended up shoveling every old person's front on the block and by the time we finished, we each had a few dollars (we didn't want to charge, but some of the old people just gave us money), mostly wrinkled old dollars that looked like they'd been under somebody's mattress for a hundred years. Clyde said his grandma used to keep money under her mattress and the dollars she gave him always smelled like mothballs. We sniffed some and sure enough— mothballs! After all that shoveling, we were so tired, Clyde just went on home and I came upstairs. Now I'm sitting by the kitchen window watching the snow and trying to be warm again.

I hope you got to play in the snow today, Lili.

Love,

Locomotion

Dear Lili,

I'm glad you like those little Polly dolls. I don't
know how anybody can get those tiny plastic
clothes on those tiny plastic bodies. I swear, those
are the tiniest dolls I've ever seen in my life, but
I'm glad I got the right thing. If they're really *all
the rage* like you say they are, then I know you
and your friends are probably playing with them
right now.

It was nice to see you get that big smile on
your face when I gave them to you. And it was
nice when you hugged me. Happy birthday, Lili.
Please tell your foster mama I said thank you again
for the lemon pound cake she sent home with us.
She really does make the best pound cakes ever. I
gave Rodney and Miss Edna some and both of
them said it was the best pound cake they'd ever
eaten. When I went to school today, I gave Clyde a
piece at lunchtime and he took a tiny bite and
then he closed his eyes and nodded. *This cake*

tastes like down south, he said. Then he ate the rest real slow because he said he wanted to keep tasting down south since he missed it there a lot. I asked him what he missed most about it and he said he missed the dirt. I looked at him like he was crazy and asked him how can you miss dirt? Clyde said he missed the way the dirt made his shoes this reddish color and when it rained, the mud wasn't brown, it was red. The red mud ran down into these ditches and made little red creeks. Clyde sat there eating that lemon pound cake and talking about that red mud to me, but his eyes had this real faraway look, like your foster mama's pound cake had taken him right back down south. It was like he never wanted that cake or that memory to end. I put my arm around his shoulder. *When me and you get big,* I said, *let's take us a bus down south.* Clyde smiled. Then he nodded and told me that was a real good idea.

**Love and Peace
and Red Dirt, Lili.**

Locomotion

Dear Lili,

Today Miss Alina said, *So when am I going to see some of that poetry you're so famous for writing?* She was handing back math tests and I got a forty on mine. That means I failed it. Real bad. I only got four out of ten right. Clyde got a hundred. He looked over at my test and said, *Man, you sure can't do math.* Miss Alina must have seen me get choky. I wasn't going to cry. Not in class. Not in front of people. But I wish, wish, wish I understood math and I don't. It goes right out of my head. Even though Clyde tries to help me and Miss Alina explains stuff again and again. I just don't get it. Clyde said it's a good thing I'm going to be a writer. He said he'd be my accountant. That made me smile a little bit. I took out my notebook and tore one of my poems out of it and gave it to Alina. She said she didn't want to take my only copy but I told her the truth, that I always make copies of my poems right after I finish writing them. (I didn't tell her I always make two copies so that I can save one for you.) She winked at me and told me she couldn't wait to read it. *Read it now,* I said. I wanted her to read it and get the bad taste of my forty percent math test out of her head. But she said, *Nope. You took the time to write it. I want to take the time to read it.* Then she put it in her folder of take-home stuff. But it's Friday, so now I gotta wait all the way until Monday to see what she thinks. But I bet she's reading it right now. Keep your fingers crossed that she likes it.

Love and Peace and Poetry,

Locomotion

Dear Lili,

It was real nice seeing you today. I'm glad we got
to go to the park. Even though it was freezing, I
loved how bright everything was and how when
me and you looked up into the sky, all we could
see was all that blue. I felt bad that your foster
mama and Miss Edna had to sit on those cold
benches and couldn't play on the swings like we
did. Miss Edna said they weren't cold though.
She'd packed that thermos of hot cider and she
said they enjoyed themselves, sitting outside in
the cold, drinking hot cider. Your foster mama
smiled a lot today. I guess she was enjoying
herself. I know you got mad when Miss Edna and
your foster mama laughed because me and you
had our hair braided the same way. Even though
you said you weren't, I know you were. Your
eyebrows get all wrinkled up when you get mad.
They weren't laughing *at* us, Lili. Miss Edna said

it just tickles her how much me and you look alike already and then we go and get the same style— and not even on purpose. It's like me and you are connected way deep. Once I read this story about these twins that never even met each other. They didn't even know each other because they'd gotten separated when they were born. But then, when they got to be grown-ups, they met and everything about them was just alike. They were even both wearing blue turtleneck sweaters! After me and Miss Edna got home, she went to take a hot bath and I sat down and reread the poem I gave Miss Alina. I added a new line. I wonder if you can guess what it is. Here's the poem, Lili. I hope you like it.

Love forever,

Locomotion

Little Things
by Lonnie C. Motion

Sometimes

Like after it snows

Or when we have Miss Edna's homemade
chicken and dumplings or

When me and my sister are sitting on the
swings at

The 9th Street playground in Prospect Park,

Just swinging a little and talking a lot,

It's hard not to think

That there's stuff in the world that's perfect

Little things people probably don't think real
hard about.

Me and Clyde having a snowball fight

Or just talking

The way pound cake makes Clyde remember
good things

The poster of the Nets that Rodney gave me

Sometimes when all the real big things feel all
*   hard and crazy*

I close my eyes and cover my ears

And think real hard

About the little things.

Dear Lili,

It's Monday night. Today Alina gave my poem
back to me and this is what she wrote.

> *Lonnie,*
> *Your poem made me think about the good*
> *things in my own life. On my list, I'd include*
> *having an amazing poet in my sixth-grade*
> *classroom. Thanks so much for sharing this*
> *with me. ☺ Alina*

☺

Lonnie

Dear Lili,

Yesterday was Miss Jamison's Check In With
Lonnie At The House Day. But when she got here,
I was just in my room and didn't feel like coming
out. She asked if she could come in and I said no
because I'd been kind of crying for a long time
and I didn't want her to see that my face was all
puffy. I heard her walk back down the hall, then I
heard her and Miss Edna talking in the kitchen.
Miss Edna said, *I do all I can to help that poor boy
be a little bit less sad*. I heard Miss Jamison ask her
why I was feeling so sad and Miss Edna said, *Well,
it **is** December*. And then Miss Jamison said, *Good
Lord, it is now, isn't it?* Then I didn't listen to them
anymore because I don't ever want to hear
anything about the month of December. I don't
want to hear about Christmas or New Year's or
Kwanzaa. Nothing. I hate December, Lili. If it
wasn't for December, Mama and Daddy would still

be alive and you and me would still be living together.

But if it wasn't for December, I would never have got to meet Miss Edna and Rodney. And you wouldn't know your foster mama. Man! I *hate* all this stuff in my head!

I'm gonna turn my brain off for a while now because Miss Edna said it was okay if I wanted to watch some TV. I'm gonna watch a whole bunch of cartoons and try to forget every single other thing.

Peace, Lili.

Locomotion

Dear Lili,

Today we had a holiday party and Miss Alina
made red and green wreath cookies and we each
got to eat two. But I couldn't eat mine because
Mama used to make cookies like that. Miss Alina
saw those cookies just sitting on my desk, so she
came over and put her hand on my shoulder. She
said real soft, *Lonnie, I'm worried about you.* I told
her I'm all right, but she looked like she didn't
believe me and the whole rest of the afternoon she
kept watching me. I wanted to tell her not to look
too close because she might see all the fire inside
of me that feels just like the fire that burned down
our house. But I just looked down at my desk and
played with my pencil. Clyde asked if he could
have my cookies and I said yeah. He asked what I
was doing for Christmas vacation and I told him
I didn't really feel like talking so he said, *That's
cool.* Then he put both cookies in his mouth at the

same time, gave me the chest pound—peace sign and walked back over to his own desk. I sat at my desk and all I could think about was how excited Mama would get around holiday time. How she'd be cooking and baking and playing Christmas music and decorating the windows. In my head I just kept seeing all that Before Time stuff and kept thinking about how the stuff that you think is going to be there always can just leave you real quick like that. Go up in flames. Be gone forever.

Lili, I don't want to write a lot about this because I don't want to pass it down to you. I don't want you worrying and remembering this stuff. I just want you to remember all the good stuff, like how Daddy used to swing us up into the air and throw us on the couch. And on the last day of school before Christmas vacation, we'd all walk down to Fulton Street where this old man used to sell real Christmas trees and Mama and Daddy would stand there while me and you walked all slow around the trees, sniffing them and feeling them and looking at each other until we decided exactly which one was perfect. And we always agreed. Then we'd go home and put our tree up and Mama would put on that song that went *Come on, baby, do the Locomotion.* And we'd all dance around the tree doing the Locomotion. Mama always used to tell us that she loved that song so much, that's why I got my name. Then she'd go on and on about how much rhythm me and you had. You loved to do that dance, Lili. I hope you haven't forgotten it.

Your brother forever,

Locomotion

Dear Lili,

Jenkins is back home. That's all I can write about
it right now. I'm sorry. I'll write more real soon.

Peace,

Locomotion

Dear Lili,

Today some men came and they worked all day
making all the doorways bigger. Like the
doorway from the kitchen to the living room and
the one from the bathroom into the hall. And
Jenkins's door. Lili, Jenkins is in a wheelchair.
Everybody's talking about his missing leg but I
don't know what it looks like because Jenkins
hasn't come out of his room and I wasn't even
here when he got here. It's been almost a week
and I've only seen little parts of him when I walk
real fast by his room. He keeps it real dark in
there and just sits in that chair staring out the
window. I don't even know what his face looks
like. Miss Edna and Rodney go in and out
bringing him food and stuff. He has a special sick
person's bathroom thing in there, so he doesn't
even come out of his room to go to the bathroom.
Last night I asked Miss Edna if there was

something I could do to help and she said, *Just be thankful he's alive and pray that my baby smiles again one day.* Miss Edna looks real tired but she also looks real relieved and it's like she got a part of her life back or something, because she goes to the store and does laundry and cooks—stuff she wasn't doing for a long time. Miss Edna said no matter what, I need to go see you on Saturday. She says she knows you miss me like crazy. Well, I miss you too, Lili. So I'll be there.

Love and Peace,

Lonnie

Dear Lili,

Today I got to see Jenkins. He wheeled himself out of the room and scared me like crazy. I didn't know he was there and when I turned around, he was just sitting in the doorway in his wheelchair. He was wearing a pair of boxing shorts. There're bandages on his left leg—I mean, on what's left of it. Jenkins just stared at me and I tried not to stare at that leg. I told him my name was Lonnie and he said, *I know that. You the boy, right?* I nodded because I figured he meant I'm the foster boy Miss Edna took in. He told me to get him some water and when I went to fill up a glass, my hand was shaking. When I brought it back to Jenkins, he drank it real fast and asked for another one. But when I got back from the kitchen with the other glass of water, he'd already gone back into his room. I didn't want to go in there, so I just dumped the water in the sink, rinsed the glass and put it in the drain. My hands were shaking the whole time.

```
Love and Peace,
Locomotion
```

Dear Lili,

Sometimes in the night, Jenkins starts yelling and
Miss Edna and Rodney go running in there to try
to calm him down. Last night he yelled, *They're
out there, Mike. I know they're out there.* I don't
know who Mike is or who is out where. Last
night, after Jenkins calmed down, I tried to go
back to sleep. I used to scream like that, Lili. Right
after the fire, I'd wake up screaming because I saw
the flames and everything. But the screaming went
away. It took a long time though. I wonder how
long it's gonna take for Jenkins.

I hope you sleep peacefully, Lili.

Love,

Locomotion

Dear Lili,

Tonight I heard a real sad conversation. I wasn't
supposed to be listening. I was supposed to be
watching television. I don't usually get to watch
TV on weeknights, but I got a ninety-seven on
my world history test and Miss Edna said I could
either have an extra dessert or watch TV for an
hour. We had ice cream for dessert and one bowl
was enough for me, so I said I wanted to watch
TV. While I was watching it, Miss Edna was
cleaning up the kitchen and I saw Jenkins go
wheelchairing past the living room. I turned the
TV down a bit. Jenkins hadn't ate dinner with
us. Usually he eats in his room and then brings
his plate into the kitchen after me, Miss Edna
and Rodney are finished. But Rodney was at a
class and so it was just me and Miss Edna
tonight. I heard Miss Edna ask Jenkins how he
was doing and I heard Jenkins's voice get all

broke sounding, so I knew he was crying.
Miss Edna was telling him to let it out. *Let all the tears you have in you come on out,* she kept saying. *It's good. It's okay.* When I used to cry a lot from remembering the fire, Miss Edna would say the same thing to me. Then Jenkins said, *I'm sorry, Mama. I'm sorry I'm broken down like this and can't help you out like I'd hoped to.* I heard Miss Edna say, *The way you helped me out was by coming home alive, honey.* You could tell she was trying to get him to believe her, but Jenkins was still crying. Neither one of them said anything for a while and all I could hear was Jenkins breathing real heavy from all the crying he was doing. Then he said, *This wasn't the dream I had, Mama.* Miss Edna said, *This wasn't the dream none of us had, but it's our lives now and we need to be living it, sweetie. We need to be living it.*

I turned the television back up and stopped listening after that. Tomorrow is Saturday and I'm going to get to see you. Miss Edna said if we wanted to go to the park, her and your foster mama will take us. I think we should ask them if we could take a walk just me and you around that loop by the lake where no matter how far away

from them we get, they can still see us. And while
we're walking, I'm going to ask you lots of
questions about your life. I want to make sure
you're living it, Lili. Make sure you're living it.

Peace,

Locomotion

Dear Lili,

The military sends different people by to see Jenkins. On Tuesdays, it's the guy that's gonna help him use his new leg when he finally gets it. Sometimes he's still here when I get home and he tells Jenkins he needs to be up trying to use his crutches. But Jenkins just tells him his leg still hurts and what's the use anyway. Sometimes I get home from school just in time to see the guy leaving. Jenkins hasn't tried to use his crutches, but the guy still comes back every week.

On Wednesdays, it's a social-worker lady who comes by to talk to Jenkins about the war. Today, she was here when I got home from school. Her voice is real soft, so most times, I can't hear her words—just the soft sound her voice makes. They were in Jenkins's room and I heard him tell her he didn't want to talk about what happened over there. I heard the lady's voice sounding kind, then

Jenkins said, *I just want to forget. I'm home now. I just want to forget.*

It's strange how there's all this stuff I'm trying to remember now and all that stuff Jenkins is trying to forget.

Peace, Lili.

Lonnie

Dear Lili,

Today Clyde came over and ate two big bowls of
spaghetti with meat sauce, two bananas, an orange,
three chocolate chip cookies and six crackers.
Clyde's skinnier than anything, so I don't know
where he puts all that food. Miss Edna watched him
put away the spaghetti and she just smiled. She said
he might be a slip of a thing now, but later on, his
muscles are going to remember that food and just
sneak up on him. That made me eat another bowl of
spaghetti because I wouldn't mind having some
muscles sneak up on me too. Jenkins came wheeling
real fast into the kitchen and yelled, *Nobody's
sneaking up on us!* His eyes were real wild. Clyde
jumped up out of his seat and that made Jenkins
scream. Miss Edna started singing, *"Seize upon that
moment long ago. One breath away and there you will
be, so young and carefree . . ."* Over and over, real
soft and slow, until Jenkins calmed down and just
dropped his head to his chest.

I felt real bad for him and started to get up and go touch his shoulder even though I was still scared of that missing leg. But Miss Edna saw me and shook her head and put her fingers to her lips. Jenkins whispered, *I'm sorry, Mama. I'm so sorry.* Clyde's eyes were wide, watching him.

Lili, I thought about your singing in church and how when I was sitting there listening to it, it felt like someone had put a warm blanket over me. How it made me feel all safe and protected from everything. I looked at Jenkins and real soft started singing a song Mama used to sing to us at night about walking in fields of gold and remembering stuff. Then I felt bad because I was singing a song about walking and Jenkins can't walk, but he looked up at me then. At first it looked like he was mad—that he thought I was making fun of him. But then, guess what, Lili? Jenkins smiled. Then Miss Edna was smiling and Clyde too. Remember when I told you there was peace in the music, Lili? It's true.

Love,

Locomotion

Dear Lili,

Today me and Angel and Eric and Clyde were all
hanging out in the school yard because Alina
gave us a math problem and said, *I know you all
don't like to do math on your lunch break, but if
just one student gets this problem right, cupcakes
for everyone.* Angel's the best at math. Next comes
Clyde. Me and Eric aren't good at all, but Eric
likes to try stuff. Before Lamont moved away,
Eric used to copy off his math tests and he'd get
real good marks. But now he gets forties like me.
But guess what? We stood in that school yard
with that math problem written on Angel's
notebook and all of us trying to figure it out for
like the whole period, and then, right before the
bell rang, Eric said, *Yo! I got it!* I'm not going to
try to explain the whole math problem to you,
because even when Eric explained it, I didn't
understand the whole thing, but he seemed real

sure. So Angel gave him a funny look but wrote down Eric's answer anyway, since he was the only one who had an answer. Then the bell rang and we went back inside and Angel gave Alina the paper. When she asked which one of us got the answer right, she looked at me like she was hoping it was me, but I pointed to Eric and her smile got big. Eric looked embarrassed, but he just shrugged, and at the end of the day, Alina gave us all cupcakes and everybody told Eric how glad they were that he'd got the problem right. Eric looked like he'd just won a million dollars with all the smiling he was doing. The cupcakes were vanilla with chocolate frosting. I ate mine real slowly. I was thinking, *It's cool that Eric doesn't need Lamont anymore to copy math from. But I still need all the help I can get.*

Love, your brother who's not good at math,

Locomotion

Dear Lili,

Today is Tuesday. When I got home from school,
Jenkins was in the living room watching TV. I tried
not to look at what's left of his leg but my eyes kept
sliding over to it. Jenkins was watching a game
show where a bunch of people were trying to win a
million dollars. When I came in, he jumped in his
wheelchair. Then, when he saw it was just me, he
went back to watching TV. I took my stuff to my
room and then came back and sat on the couch. For
a little while, we just watched the show together
without saying anything. Miss Edna came in from
the kitchen and gave me two chocolate chip cookies
and a glass of milk. I said thank you and offered
Jenkins one of the cookies. He looked at me for a
second, then took both of them. Then he smiled
and put one back on my plate and said, *Gotcha!*
That made me smile. When Jenkins smiles, I can
see the old Jenkins inside of him. The Jenkins that's
in the pictures. But he doesn't smile that much.

After the millionaire show went off, another

game show came on. Jenkins asked if I'd get him another cookie, so I went in the kitchen. Miss Edna whispered, *He doing okay?* And I said yeah. She gave me two more cookies. When I came back into the living room, the TV was off and Jenkins was just staring out the living room window. We ate our cookies without saying anything, then Jenkins asked me if I missed my people. At first, I wasn't sure what he was talking about, but then I realized he was asking about you and Mama and Daddy. I shrugged and Jenkins said shrugging doesn't mean anything because it means too many things, so I whispered yeah. Jenkins kept staring out the window. *You've had a hard life, huh?* he said. It wasn't really a question, so I didn't answer it. Jenkins said every time somebody thinks they've had a hard life, they come along and meet somebody whose life's been just a little bit harder. He turned his whole wheelchair around so that he was looking right at me. *Mama says you're a real good kid,* he said. I shrugged, but then I didn't want him to think that was all I did, so I said, *That's cool.* Jenkins said, *Yeah, cool.*

Peace, Lili.

Locomotion

Dear Lili,

This morning when I woke up, the sun was out.
And when I opened the kitchen window, the air
coming in wasn't so cold anymore. While I stood
at the window breathing in the almost-warm air,
Jenkins came into the kitchen. He said what's up,
and I said what's up, then he wheeled his chair to
the kitchen table where Miss Edna had left him a
plate of waffles and eggs and started eating.

I sat across from him and started eating my
own breakfast. Jenkins dropped his fork and I
bent down to get it for him and couldn't help but
stare at his half leg, sitting there under the table
with his whole one. I'd read a story where the guy
lost his leg but he still felt like it was there and
sometimes he'd get up at night thinking he still
had two legs and try to walk across the room and
fall down. Jenkins must have known I was down
there staring because he said, *It ain't coming back*.
I got up real fast, rinsed his fork off for him and

handed it back. But I didn't say anything. Jenkins poured syrup on his waffles, took a bite and chewed real slowly. After he swallowed, he said, *But I'm alive. And that's supposed to be what matters.*

I told him Miss Edna's real glad to have him home. He said she's his mama so she's supposed to be glad. *We're all glad,* I said. Jenkins stared at me for a long time. His looking at me that way made me nervous, so I went back to eating. Then he asked how come I was glad when I didn't even know him. I didn't know what to say because I wanted to say *I do know you* but I didn't.

I just kept eating my breakfast. *'Cause you were over there fighting for us,* I said. *And your mama said you don't even like fighting.* Jenkins said, *Nobody should be over there fighting, you know that, right?* I shrugged because I didn't know what to think about the war anymore. At school, some of the kids talked about how great it was and how we were winning and all. But Clyde said it wasn't a good war, that we didn't even need to be in it but we were. And then every day there were news reports about people dying or coming home like Jenkins. The other day, Miss Edna was reading a news article and there were all these letters from guys who had died. Some of them knew they were gonna die and other ones were just talking about how scared they were over there. One guy wrote, *Things explode all around me and every time something explodes somebody dies. I wonder when it's gonna be my turn.* And the next week, the article said, he was dead. I said to Jenkins, *I don't know about everybody else but I know I don't like fighting.* He asked me why not, and I said, *I just don't, that's all.*

Yeah, Jenkins said. *I just don't either, Li'l Bro.*

Jenkins finished his breakfast, then rolled himself away from the table. He took both his hands and lifted his half leg up. He still had his thigh and maybe his knee, but that part was all covered with bandages, so I wasn't sure. When he lifted it up, he made a face like it hurt.

I could hear Rodney in the bathroom singing, "On top of Old Smoky . . ."

A building fell on it, Jenkins said like I'd asked him how he lost it or something. He was looking at his leg but he was talking to me. *I know you been wondering.* I asked him if it hurt a lot. *Only now,* he said. *When it happened, I passed out. By the time I was halfway conscious again, the leg was gone.* He put it down again and massaged his bandaged knee. *It was like something right out of* The Wizard of Oz. Then he looked at me and smiled. It was a nice smile—real peaceful like in those pictures of him from back in the day. *I guess I'm not the Wicked Witch though, because then that building would have landed on my whole body, huh?* I smiled then. *You get a medal when you lose a part of your body*, Jenkins said. *Not like I can pin that medal to my knee and get up and walk again though.* He said after they give you the medal, you get to go home. In my head I was thinking about what Clyde said—about how the people over there get all used up. I didn't want Jenkins to be all used up. I wanted him to be one hundred percent Jenkins again.

Rodney came into the kitchen, but Jenkins didn't see him because his back was to the kitchen door. Rodney said what's up and Jenkins jumped in his wheelchair and Rodney apologized to him, then came over and gave Jenkins a quick what's-up hug. He gave me one too. Rodney was wearing his work clothes and smelled like cologne. One time I took some of it and wore it to school and all the girls said I smelled like a cologne factory and I needed to figure out how to wear that stuff so I didn't smell up the whole school. Rodney poured himself some coffee and asked Jenkins what his plan for the day was. *I'm going for a run,* Jenkins said. Then he looked at me and winked. *You still think you funny, Jenks,* Rodney said. But you could tell he was happy to hear Jenkins cracking a joke.

This kid is cool, Jenkins said, pointing to me.

You think I don't know that? Rodney said. *All the living me and him been doing.*

They both looked at me. I looked down at my plate and smiled real big.

Peace, Lili.

Locomotion

Dear Lili,

Some days, Rodney is the student teacher for third-graders at P.S. 377 on the other side of Brooklyn. He said the kids in his school are nice but sometimes they get real crazy. Rodney's real patient, so I bet the kids like him. And he's patient when he's trying to teach you something, so I bet the kids are learning a whole lot. Tonight I was in the living room doing my homework when he got home and he asked me if I needed any help. I told him I didn't because for the first time in a long time, I understood all my homework! *Man,* Rodney said, *I'm useless around here!* He went into the kitchen and Miss Edna asked him how was his day. I heard him say, *It is what it is, Mama,* then I heard the refrigerator door open and close and Rodney came back in the living room with a ginger ale. Jenkins wheeled himself into the living room. He was wearing a white T-shirt and some

new-looking jeans and had a book on his lap.
Rodney saw him and asked him what it was. Then
Jenkins told him the name of the book and started
telling him what it was about. Rodney sat down
on the couch and they talked back and forth about
the book and I could tell that when they were
teenagers, they probably did this kind of talking
all the time. It was a grown-up novel about a boy
who grows up with a mean stepfather or
something. I wasn't that interested in the book, so
I went back to my homework. But I liked the way
their voices sounded, kind of quiet, just going
back and forth. Miss Edna was making beef stew
and the whole house smelled good. Rodney asked
Jenkins how his leg was doing. Jenkins said, *I
don't know, it ain't here anymore.* I thought he was
mad but then they both started laughing. Miss
Edna came out of the kitchen and asked what all
the laughing was about and Rodney said, *I don't
know, Mama. You the one who said sometimes you
gotta laugh to keep from crying.* And Jenkins said,
And sometimes you just gotta laugh.

It's true, Lili. Sometimes you do have to laugh
to keep from crying. And sometimes the world
feels all right and good and kind of like it's

becoming nice again around you. And you realize it, and realize how happy you are in it, and you just gotta laugh.

There's peace at our house tonight, Lili. I hope there's some at your house too.

Locomotion

Dear Lili,

Today when I got home from school, Jenkins was in the living room. He had his crutches and he was taking real slow steps around the room with them. Those crutches been sitting outside his room for a long time but he never wanted to use them. He always said *This wheelchair is fine!* but when he said it, you knew it was because he was mad that he had to use *anything,* let alone some crutches. He's so tall, Lili! I couldn't believe it. I just stood there looking up at him. And when he saw me, he said, *This is hard, Li'l Brother, but I'm gonna do it*. Then he took some more small steps and sat back down in his wheelchair with a real tired sigh. *I just gotta keep practicing,* he said. *Gotta keep on keeping on.* Then he cursed real soft and dropped his head into his hands. I told him if he wanted to, I could help him get in and out of the wheelchair and up onto the crutches. I really didn't know if I was strong enough to help someone as big as Jenkins, but I sure did want to try. The way I figured it, Jenkins and Miss Edna and Rodney'd helped me a lot and it wasn't a whole lot to help him, but it was something. I know they're not expecting any kind of payback, but it felt real good to think that maybe there was something I could do in the family. I didn't know if Jenkins heard me at first, but then after a minute passed, he lifted his head, nodded and told me I was a good kid and that most likely, he'd take me up on my offer. My body's getting stronger every day, so I'm ready to try. ☺

Love,

Locomotion

Dear Lili,

A few days ago, Miss Edna took some pictures of me, Rodney and Jenkins. Me and Rodney were sitting on the couch and Jenkins was in his wheelchair. Miss Edna said, *I can't believe I'm going to finally have some pictures of my three favorite men.*

And guess what? Today we got the pictures back. Miss Edna waited until we was all sitting down for dinner before she pulled them out. She said, *I got something I think is going to crack a smile out of the hardest nut.* Then she showed us the pictures and there was Jenkins, not even smiling one bit but giving me rabbit ears!

We laughed for a long, long time.

**Love and Peace and
Rabbit Ears,**

Locomotion

Dear Lili,

When Jenkins leans on me to get out of that
wheelchair and onto those crutches, it's like there's
a giant on my shoulders. And sometimes it feels
like I'm just gonna fall right down under all that
weight. But I don't, Lili. I stay standing.
I stay standing.

Peace, Lili.

Locomotion

Dear Lili,

This morning when I was walking to school, I saw Miss Shore's crocuses pushing up out of the dirt. I stopped to look at them and she came out of her house. I thought she was going to chase me away with her broom, but she didn't even have it with her. She asked me what I was looking at and I told her I was looking at her flowers. *Those are crocuses,* she said. I wanted to say *I know* because if there's one flower I know, it's crocuses. When we were little, Mama used to always point them out to us. She'd say *Spring's coming.* And sometimes I'd laugh and tell her it's too cold for spring to be coming. And then she'd point and show me the shoots coming up out of the ground. *Crocuses, Lonnie,* she'd say. *That's always the first sign.*

That's the first sign of spring, I said to Miss Shore.

Miss Shore gave me a look—like she thought I was making fun of her. But then she smiled and said, *It sure is. And it can't come a moment too soon now, can it?*

Spring's coming, Lili. Rodney said spring is usually the most peaceful time. So I guess all that praying for Peace me and you did is finally paying off.

I could feel Miss Shore watching me walk down the block. But her eyes on my back didn't feel mean. They felt warm. Like she was watching me and watching over me at the same time. When I got to the end of the block, I took a deep breath and looked up into the sky. It was real blue and real clear. It made me think that somewhere not too far away from us, Peace was coming. Slowly. But it was on its way.

Love and Peace,

Locomotion

Imagine Peace Again

I think it's your family

And your friends like Clyde holding the ball
out to you

And letting you take that extra shot.

I think Peace is springtime and your whole
family

Having a picnic after your brother Jenkins

Has walked

down three flights of stairs

With just his crutches and

That big grin he gets these days because

He's happy

To be alive. Imagine

Peace is that moment when

Rodney and Jenkins both

Stare up at the blue sky

And watery sun.

Peace is your sister running to you at Prospect
 Park,

Throwing her arms around you and saying

I've missed you a million, Lonnie.

Peace is the good stuff

That happens to all of us

Sometimes.

Lonnie Collins Motion

PEACE, LOCOMOTION

Discussion Questions

- What is a family? Is family important? Explain. Clyde tells Lonnie that "There's all kinds of mamas" (page 35), Lili tells Lonnie that she wants the Mama she used to have and the Mama she has now (page 64). Lonnie is at first skeptical of their ideas about mothers. What do you think?

- Have you experienced a teacher like Ms. Cooper or Miss Alina? Describe your experience. What do you think Rodney would be like as a teacher?

- Why would Miss Alina say to try to write, think, or talk about one true thing every day (page 42)? Do you agree that this is a worthwhile goal?

- What do you imagine peace to be? Is Lonnie's idea about peace on page 77 possible: "everyone putting down their weapons and no more wars anywhere"?

- In one letter to Lili, Lonnie comments on wants and needs (pages 86–87). What's the difference between a want and a need? What does Lonnie want? What does he need? What do you want? What do you need?

- Clyde is Lonnie's best friend. What are the qualities you look for in a friend or a best friend? Does everyone have to have a best friend? Why or why not?

- Consider Lonnie's poem "Little Things" on page 96. What does the poem mean to you? What little things are important to you?

- Miss Edna encourages Jenkins to be living life (page 111), and Lonnie writes to Lili that he wants to make sure she is living her life. What does it mean to be living life? Do you think you are living your life?

- What does the saying "sometimes you gotta laugh to keep from crying" mean (page 127)? Do you agree or disagree?

- If you could ask Lonnie one question, what would it be?

- What do you think happens to Lonnie? What do you imagine his life will be like in ten years?

Turn the page for a look
at JACQUELINE WOODSON's
National Book Award Finalist

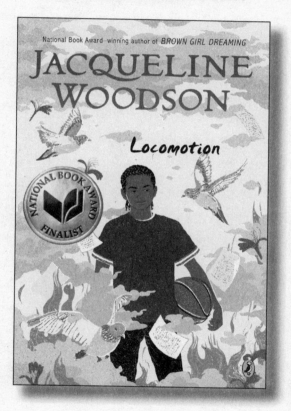

Poem Book

This whole book's a poem 'cause every time I try to
tell the whole story my mind goes *Be quiet!*
Only it's not my mind's voice,
it's Miss Edna's over and over and over
Be quiet!

I'm not a really loud kid, I swear. I'm just me and
sometimes I maybe make a little bit of noise.
If I was a grown-up maybe Miss Edna
wouldn't always be telling me to be quiet
but I'm eleven and maybe eleven's just noisy.

Maybe twelve's quieter.

But when Miss Edna's voice comes on, the ideas in my
head go out like a candle and all you see left is this little
string of smoke that disappears real quick
before I even have a chance to find out
what it's trying to say.

So this whole book's a poem because poetry's short and

this whole book's a poem 'cause Ms. Marcus says
write it down before it leaves your brain.
I tell her about the smoke and she says
Good, Lonnie, write that.
Not a whole lot of people be saying *Good, Lonnie* to me

so I write the string-of-smoke thing down real fast.
Ms. Marcus says *We'll worry about line breaks later.*

Write fast, Lonnie, Ms. Marcus says.
And I'm thinking Yeah, I better write fast before Miss
Edna's voice comes on and blows my candle idea out.

Roof

At night sometimes after Miss Edna goes to bed I go
up on the roof
Sometimes I sit counting the stars
Maybe one is my mama and
another one is my daddy And maybe that's why
sometimes they flicker a bit
I mean *the stars* flicker

Line Break
Poem

Ms. Marcus
says
line breaks help
us figure out
what matters
to the poet
Don't jumble your ideas
Ms. Marcus says
Every line
should count.

Memory

Once when we was real
little
I was sitting at the window holding my baby sister, Lili
on my lap.
Mama was in the kitchen and Daddy must've
been at work.
Mama kept saying
Honey, don't you drop my baby.

A pigeon came flying over to the ledge
and was looking at us.
Lili put her hand on the glass and the pigeon tried
to peck at it.
Lili snatched her hand away and screamed.
Not a scared scream,
just one of those laughing screams
that babies who can't talk yet like to do.

Mama came running out the kitchen
drying her hands on her jeans.
When she saw us just sitting there, she let out a breath.
Oh, my Lord, she said,
I thought you'd dropped my baby.
I asked
Was I ever your baby, Mama?
and Mama looked at me all warm and smiley.

You still are, she said.
Then she went back in the kitchen.

I felt safe then.
I held Lili tighter.
Maybe if I was eleven then
and if one of my friends had been around,
I would have been embarrassed, I guess.
But I was just a little kid
and nobody else was around.
Just me and Lili and Mama and the pigeons.
And outside the sun
getting bright and warm suddenly
like it'd been listening in.

Mama

Some days, like today
and yesterday and probably
tomorrow—all my missing gets jumbled up inside of me.

You know honeysuckle talc powder?
Mama used to smell like that. She told me
honeysuckle's really a flower but all I know
is the powder that smells like Mama.
Sometimes when the missing gets real bad
I go to the drugstore and before the guard starts
following me around like I'm gonna steal something
I go to the cosmetics lady and ask her if she has it.
When she says yeah, I say
Can I smell it to see if it's the right one?
Even though the cosmetics ladies roll their eyes at me
they let me smell it.
And for those few seconds, Mama's alive
again.
And I'm remembering
all kinds of good things about her like
the way she laughed at my jokes
even when they were dumb
and the way she sometimes just grabbed me
and hugged me before
I had a chance to get away.

And the way her voice always sounded good
and bad at the same time when she was singing
in the shower.
And her red pocketbook that always had some
tangerine Life Savers inside it for me and Lili

No, I say to the cosmetics lady. *It's not the right one.*
And then I leave fast.
Before somebody asks to check my pockets
which are always empty 'cause I don't steal.

Lili

And sometimes I combed Lili's hair
braids mostly but sometimes a ponytail.
Lili would cry sometimes
the kind of crying where no tears came out.
Big faker.
I wouldn't't've hurt her head for a million dollars.

Some days
like today and yesterday and probably tomorrow
that's all that's on my mind
Mama and Lili.

Hair and honeysuckle talc powder.

First

First Miss Edna turned the key and
opened her door for me
and said *This ain't much, but it's all I have.*
A living room, a kitchen with a table and three chairs,
a room with just a bed in it and a poster of Dr. J
when he still played for the Sixers and had an Afro.
You'll sleep in here, she said.
Another room down the hall.
No need for you to ever go in there, she said.
I never did.

All along the living room walls there's pictures
of her sons. Grown-up and gone now.

I used to fill up Miss Edna's house with noise.

I used to talk all the time.
I used to laugh real loud and holler especially
when the Knicks won a game 'cause
that don't happen too much.

Be quiet! Miss Edna said.
Hush, Lonnie, Miss Edna said.
Shhhh, Lonnie, Miss Edna said.
Children should be seen but not heard, Miss Edna said.

And my voice got quieter
and quieter
and quiet.

Now some days Miss Edna looks at me and says
You need to smile more, Lonnie.
You need to laugh sometimes
maybe make a little noise.
Where's that boy I used to know,
the one who couldn't be quiet?

Turn the page for a look
at JACQUELINE WOODSON's
moving story of her childhood.

Winner of the National Book Award
Coretta Scott King Award winner
Newbery Honor winner

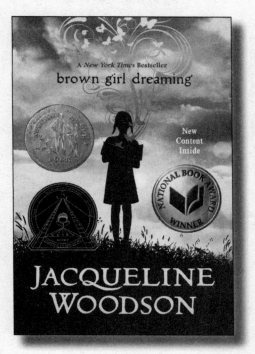

"Gorgeous." —*Vanity Fair*

"This is a book full of poems that cry out to be learned by heart. These are poems that will, for years to come, be stored in our bloodstream."
—*The New York Times Book Review*

"Moving and resonant . . . captivating."
—*The Wall Street Journal*

"A radiantly warm memoir." —*The Washington Post*

february 12, 1963

I am born on a Tuesday at University Hospital
Columbus, Ohio,
USA—
a country caught

between Black and White.

I am born not long from the time
or far from the place
where
my great-great-grandparents
worked the deep rich land
unfree
dawn till dusk
unpaid
drank cool water from scooped-out gourds
looked up and followed
the sky's mirrored constellation
to freedom.

I am born as the South explodes,
too many people too many years

enslaved, then emancipated
but not free, the people
who look like me
keep fighting
and marching
and getting killed
so that today—
February 12, 1963
and every day from this moment on,
brown children like me can grow up
free. Can grow up
learning and voting and walking and riding
wherever *we* want.

I am born in Ohio but
the stories of South Carolina already run
like rivers
through my veins.

second daughter's
second day on earth

My birth certificate says: Female Negro
Mother: Mary Anne Irby, 22, Negro
Father: Jack Austin Woodson, 25, Negro

In Birmingham, Alabama, Martin Luther King Jr.
   is planning a march on Washington, where
John F. Kennedy is president.
In Harlem, Malcolm X is standing on a soapbox
   talking about a revolution.

> *Outside the window of University Hospital,*
> *snow is slowly falling. So much already*
> *covers this vast Ohio ground.*

In Montgomery, only seven years have passed
   since Rosa Parks refused
to give up
her seat on a city bus.

> *I am born brown-skinned, black-haired*
> *and wide-eyed.*
> *I am born Negro here and Colored there*

and somewhere else,
the Freedom Singers have linked arms,
their protests rising into song:
Deep in my heart, I do believe
that we shall overcome someday.

and somewhere else, James Baldwin
is writing about injustice, each novel,
each essay, changing the world.

        I do not yet know who I'll be
        what I'll say
        how I'll say it . . .

Not even three years have passed since a brown girl
named Ruby Bridges
walked into an all-white school.
Armed guards surrounded her while hundreds
of white people spat and called her names.

She was six years old.

        I do not know if I'll be strong like Ruby.
        I do not know what the world will look like
        when I am finally able to walk, speak, write . . .
        Another Buckeye!
        the nurse says to my mother.
        Already, I am being named for this place.

Ohio. The Buckeye State.
My fingers curl into fists, automatically
This is the way, *my mother said,*
of every baby's hand.
I do not know if these hands will become
Malcolm's—raised and fisted
or Martin's—open and asking
or James's—curled around a pen.
I do not know if these hands will be
Rosa's
or Ruby's
gently gloved
and fiercely folded
calmly in a lap,
on a desk,
around a book,
ready
to change the world . . .

a girl named jack

Good enough name for me, my father said
the day I was born.
Don't see why
she can't have it, too.

But the women said no.
My mother first.
Then each aunt, pulling my pink blanket back
patting the crop of thick curls
tugging at my new toes
touching my cheeks.

We won't have a girl named Jack, my mother said.

And my father's sisters whispered,
A boy named Jack was bad enough.
But only so my mother could hear.
Name a girl Jack, my father said,
and she can't help but
grow up strong.
Raise her right, my father said,
and she'll make that name her own.

6

Name a girl Jack
and people will look at her twice, my father said.

For no good reason but to ask if her parents
were crazy, my mother said.

And back and forth it went until I was Jackie
and my father left the hospital mad.

My mother said to my aunts,
Hand me that pen, wrote
Jacqueline where it asked for a name.
Jacqueline, just in case
someone thought to drop the *ie.*

Jacqueline, just in case
I grew up and wanted something a little bit longer
and further away from
Jack.

the woodsons of ohio

My father's family
can trace their history back
to Thomas Woodson of Chillicothe, said to be
the first son
of Thomas Jefferson and Sally Hemings
some say
this isn't so but . . .

the Woodsons of Ohio know
what the Woodsons coming before them
left behind, in Bibles, in stories,
in history coming down through time

so

ask any Woodson why
you can't go down the Woodson line
without
finding
doctors and lawyers and teachers
athletes and scholars and people in government
they'll say,

We had a head start.
They'll say,
Thomas Woodson expected the best of us.
They'll lean back, lace their fingers
across their chests,
smile a smile that's older than time, say,

Well it all started back before Thomas Jefferson
Woodson of Chillicothe . . .

and they'll begin to tell our long, long story.

the ghosts of the
nelsonville house

The Woodsons are one
of the few Black families in this town, their house
is big and white and sits
on a hill.

Look up
to see them
through the high windows
inside a kitchen filled with the light
of a watery Nelsonville sun. In the parlor
a fireplace burns warmth
into the long Ohio winter.

Keep looking and it's spring again,
the light's gold now, and dancing
across the pine floors.

Once, there were so many children here
running through this house
up and down the stairs, hiding under beds
and in trunks,

sneaking into the kitchen for tiny pieces
of icebox cake, cold fried chicken,
thick slices of their mother's honey ham . . .

Once, my father was a baby here
and then he was a boy . . .

But that was a long time ago.

In the photos my grandfather is taller than everybody
and my grandmother just an inch smaller.

On the walls their children run through fields,
    play in pools,
dance in teen-filled rooms, all of them

grown up and gone now—
but wait!

Look closely:

There's Aunt Alicia, the baby girl,
curls spiraling over her shoulders, her hands
cupped around a bouquet of flowers. Only
four years old in that picture, and already,
a reader.

Beside Alicia another picture, my father, Jack,

the oldest boy.
Eight years old and mad about something
or is it someone
we cannot see?

In another picture, my uncle Woody,
baby boy
laughing and pointing
the Nelsonville house behind him and maybe
his brother at the end of his pointed finger.

My aunt Anne in her nurse's uniform,
my aunt Ada in her university sweater
Buckeye to the bone . . .

The children of Hope and Grace.

Look closely. There I am
in the furrow of Jack's brow,
in the slyness of Alicia's smile,
in the bend of Grace's hand . . .

There I am . . .

Beginning.

it'll be scary
sometimes

My great-great-grandfather on my father's side
was born free in Ohio,

1832.

Built his home and farmed his land,
then dug for coal when the farming
wasn't enough. Fought hard
in the war. His name in stone now
on the Civil War Memorial:

William J. Woodson
United States Colored Troops,
Union, Company B 5th Regt.

A long time dead but living still
among the other soldiers
on that monument in Washington, D.C.

His son was sent to Nelsonville
lived with an aunt

William Woodson
the only brown boy in an all-white school.

You'll face this in your life someday,
my mother will tell us
over and over again.
A moment when you walk into a room and

no one there is like you.

It'll be scary sometimes. But think of William Woodson
and you'll be all right.